Saraband for Shadows

Saraband
for Shadows

Geoffrey Trease

M

First published 1982 by
MACMILLAN CHILDREN'S BOOKS
A division of Macmillan Publishers Limited
London and Basingstoke

Associated companies throughout the world

Photoset, printed and bound in Great Britain by
REDWOOD BURN LIMITED
Trowbridge, Wiltshire

British Library Cataloguing in Publication Data
Trease, Geoffrey
  Saraband for shadows.
  I. Title
  823'.914 [J]   PZ7

ISBN 0–333–32848–5

Contents

One *Castle in the Air*

Suddenly – he could not think why – he felt glad of the sword that joggled at his hip as they clattered across the hump of the bridge.

Since taking service with Mandeville, Anthony had developed something of his master's uncanny nose for hidden dangers. Such an instinct was useful. If you worked for Mad Mandeville you were apt to find yourself in awkward places.

Oddly though, at this moment, that young gentleman himself showed no sign of uneasiness. He was giving his full attention to Lord Ravenwood's flow of explanation. Riding a respectful yard or two behind, Anthony was near enough to study the two friends' faces constantly turning to each other – those two so very different profiles, Mandeville's swarthy, eagle-sharp, and his lordship's so chubby and ruddy, like a ripe pippin.

"Yes, you'll see a mighty change, Renold. I've been busy while you've been on your travels, I can tell you!"

And you *are* telling him, thought Anthony with a smile. Lord Ravenwood had scarcely paused for breath since their arrival last night, weary after five days on the road from London. It had been dark by then, too late to view the new buildings. This morning, though, when an extra hour between the sheets would have been welcome, nothing would satisfy him but that they should rise in the chilly spring dawn and join him on his usual ride of inspection.

Anthony longed to spur forward, pluck his master's sleeve, and murmur his misgivings. But of course he dared not. A nobody did not interrupt a nobleman without good cause. And what cause could he give for this utterly vague, irrational foreboding?

He turned in his saddle to reassure himself that at least Tobias was following. And he was. But the rascal was so deep in gossip with my lord's old groom that he was deaf and blind to everything else. Boasting as usual. Holding forth to this goggling countryman about his exploits in far-off lands.

Only Anthony himself, riding along between the two couples, the masters and their men, was outside both conversations, undistracted and alert.

Yet alert for what, in Heaven's name?

This was not France or Italy, not even his own London, where, as he well knew, the byways held their share of menace. This was peaceful Herefordshire, only a few miles short of Mandeville's own home, their journey's end. And Lord Ravenwood had been Mandeville's friend since they were boys together.

Certainly no danger from *that* quarter. Ravenwood was a man to trust. Anthony had liked him from the first minutes of his kindly welcome last night. My lord might be a very great gentleman – Tobias whispered that he was one of the wealthiest in the kingdom, with his vast estates, his coal and iron, his stone-quarries and his well-timbered woods. But he had had a smile and a word for the unimportant youth from London, and some mysterious old joke for Tobias. Even this morning, as they passed a milkmaid with her pails amid the blotchy-faced Herefordshire cows, he had broken off to call a cheerful good-morning, sweeping off his plumed hat in answer to her curtsey as though she had been the greatest lady in the land.

Now he was talking again about his schemes. In this quiet country place it was not every day he had a friend to share them with. Mandeville, who had seen so much more of the world, was the perfect listener.

Ravenwood was driven by a dream. It was to rebuild – utterly, and to a new design – the castle of his ancestors.

A hundred years ago the old stronghold had been in decay. It had outlived its purpose. The Welsh wars were an ancient memory, England herself had found peace at last under the Tudor kings. The dark and discomfort of a crumbling fortress offered no attractions as a home.

It was then that Henry VIII had closed down the monasteries throughout his kingdom. Down in the valley, on the opposite bank of the river, stood Crucorney Priory in just the sort of idyllic setting that the Cistercian monks had always preferred for their houses. The remaining Brothers had been pensioned off and sent away. The buildings, and the well-farmed lands that surrounded them, had been taken by the King. He, far away in London, had been glad to sell them to the Lord Ravenwood of the day. He, in his turn, had been happy to leave the draughts of Crucorney Castle and move down into the Priory, which was already more comfortable and convenient, and could easily be improved to make it a home worthy of a nobleman.

And so it had become, by the standards of that age. Indeed Anthony, sleeping under its roof last night, had thought it still fine enough for anyone. But my lord had other ideas, and over supper he had poured them out to his guests.

What had been splendid when completed in the first years of Queen Elizabeth was now hopelessly old-fashioned for the era of King Charles. Lord Ravenwood was determined to build a new home that should rank among the great houses of the kingdom.

"We had a clear choice," he had explained, his blue eyes sparkling in the candlelight. "Pull down this place and rebuild. Or clear the old castle ruins and use the site." He had chuckled, smiling at his wife. "My lady of course decided."

"My lady did nothing of the sort," Lady Ravenwood had retorted good-temperedly. "I love the Priory and should be happy to stay here. Certainly I could not bear to see it pulled down – and where should we live while it was being built up again? No, if my lord is set on this fancy, let it *be* a castle in the air. Then the children and I can stay snug in the house we know until the other is ready to move into."

"Which will not be as long as you think, Rose! The work is going excellently."

"I can't wait to see it," Mandeville had interjected politely.

"And I can't wait to hear what you think of it!"

Hence the early call, the horses saddled ready in the yard, their steamy breath mingling with the fog of dawn. And now they were riding along the opposite bank of the mountain river that boiled so whitely round boulders smooth as giant eggs, bubbling and chuckling (thought Anthony) as his lordship did himself.

The hills loomed as vague presences, scarcely visible through the mist. This did nothing to make Anthony feel easier. He liked to see where he was going. He did not care for this sensation of riding into the unknown. And yet, he told himself impatiently for the third time, such apprehension was absurd.

Mandeville was not at this moment involved in any matter likely to create dangers. Anthony was sure of that – or as sure as anybody could be, with a master as devious and reserved as Mandeville. This journey to Herefordshire was no more than a duty visit, long overdue, to his mother. And though admittedly Mandeville had a few enemies scattered about the world, it would be surprising if any were lurking for him in this remote place.

"There you are!"

Ravenwood's triumphant shout startled him from his anxious broodings. His lordship drew rein, one gauntleted hand upflung, pointing.

The others halted, bunching behind him, staring upwards.

The first beams of sunrise, slanting across the lower hills to the east, were beginning to disperse the mist. Ragged scarves of vapour trailed across the tree-clothed precipice immediately in front of them, unravelling lazily until, like a face unveiled, the fantastic turrets and battlements of the new Crucorney swam into view, palest gold.

Anthony caught his breath. In that instant Ravenwood's fantasy cast its spell upon him.

True, the structure was smaller than he had expected.

It reminded him of the sham fortress he had seen at a masque ouside London when he was a child – a wonderful, unforgettable spectacle. It had been only painted canvas, his father had explained to him, stretched on a timber frame, a flimsy make-believe. There had been a garrison of shrieking, giggling court ladies, pelting with roses the elegant gentlemen who pretended to besiege them. But at a distance, in the torchlight, that airy Castle of Love had seemed to him, as a little boy, unspeakably beautiful.

Now, seeming to float upon a foam of mist, peach-tinted by the sunrise, Crucorney looked just such a fairy fortress – one that would never know the smell of gunpowder, save what was needed for a firework display.

Mandeville said something. Ravenwood answered.

"Oh, it is only what we call 'the Little Castle', where we shall have our private family apartments. The main buildings will stretch all along the ridge, with a terrace below. I look to you to find me some antique statues from Italy."

"I'll do my best, Will."

"Ah, the mist is clearing. You can see the Great

Gallery. It will be seventy yards long when it's finished. With ten tall windows—"

Anthony followed his lordship's pointing finger. To the right of the Little Castle, linked to it by a battlemented walk, the long façade ran along the skyline, still roofless, with tall scaffold poles standing like lances against the drifting clouds. The inner walls had not yet risen so high – the empty air was framed white in the unglazed windows, which faced the world below like so many blind eye-sockets.

But – Anthony wondered – *were* they so blind?

Or had he, for a few moments, seen the straight line of the third window-ledge broken by the blob of a human head? He peered intently, instinctively rising in his stirrups. The blob had gone. But he would have sworn it had been there before. It had vanished now. So, it was something that moved, almost certainly something that was alive. A perched bird on the ledge, which had taken off again? He had seen no flap of wings. Far more likely a man. Someone watching their approach.

There was, of course, a likely explanation. Masons already at work up there. If it was Lord Ravenwood's regular habit to visit the site before breakfast, the men would keep an eye open for his coming.

To satisfy himself, he turned to the groom behind.

"Are they working up there now?" he inquired casually.

"Oh, no, sir. Not today. They're still held up for the stone."

Thomas plunged into explanations. His lordship had his own quarries a mile or two away. They supplied much of the stone, just as all the timber was cut in his own woods, the lime and the bricks prepared in different parts of the estate. The new castle, boasted the old man, would be built entirely from his lordship's own materials.

Anthony barely listened. "I think I saw someone up there," he said.

"Oh, no, sir." The groom shook his head. He was positive. "You see, there's nothing they can do this morning, sir. Not till they get another waggonload."

Anthony remained unsatisfied. He must somehow speak to Mandeville, the merest hint to put him on guard.

He was too late, however. Ravenwood and Mandeville had dismounted. Ravenwood was saying, "Shall we go up then?" Mandeville made some laughing reference to their boyhood days, when they had raced each other up the steep hillside – and Ravenwood answered with a challenge. Without more ado, the two gentlemen were off.

Taken by surprise, Anthony hesitated, uncertain whether to follow them. Then, still haunted by that unaccountable presentiment that all was not quite as it should be, he dropped lightly to the ground.

"His lordship always likes me to wait here for him," said the groom quickly.

And Tobias said, in a tactful warning tone: "Sir Renold and his lordship have not seen each other these two years past."

"I know. And I know my place – I shan't intrude upon them." Anthony heard his own voice, curter and more irritable than he had meant it to be. It was the anxiety he could not explain. "My place is with Sir Renold," he said with dignity, and realised that he was sounding pompous.

"Have it your own way, then," said Tobias, adding with good-humoured irony, "Thomas and I are only humble serving men. *Our* place is to wait here and hold horses for the gentlemen." His Welsh lilt, never absent, had grown more marked since they entered the border country.

Anthony made no answer. He felt rebuked, angry with himself, and more uncertain than ever. Action gave welcome relief to that uncertainty. He started up the zigzag path.

The two young men were already well above him. Mandeville, in his cloak of Vandyke brown, was hard to see amid the stippled haze of the still wintry woodland that clung to the hill-face. But his lordship's cape was as red as his cheeks. It fluttered like a banner between the dangling hazel catkins. Ravenwood, knowing the track from daily use, was panting upwards several yards in front of Mandeville.

No risk of intruding upon his betters at this stage, thought Anthony, stumbling in their wake. Indeed, if the muddy track had not been so well trodden, he might easily have lost them. No voices, no laughter, floated down. The runners needed all their breath for the climb.

Thank heaven, the top! The fringe of treetops above him gave place to the irregular line of the unfinished Great Gallery. A few more paces. More of the façade rose into view, the tall window-spaces, the slender flat pilasters paired off between them, the niches left vacant for statues... Yes, a veritable palace, no doubt, his lordship was raising on this remote westland hill. But Anthony's mind was not on architecture.

He came out on what would one day be the terrace, broad but as yet unpaved and unbalustraded, littered with heaps of building material, empty wheelbarrows and ladders.

Of Ravenwood and Mandeville there was no sign. He saw at once which way they must have gone.

In the centre of the long frontage yawned a magnificent arched opening. There, eventually, would be the main doors of the gallery, with a stairway leading up from the terrace. The stairs were not yet built. The arch gaped empty, six feet above a sheer drop. The workmen had rigged up an arrangement of slanting planks to wheel their barrows up and down. This, for the present, was the quickest route into the rest of the site.

Anthony ran lightly up the sagging planks. It was a time to watch one's footing, and it was only when he was a few paces short of the archway that he lifted his eyes and saw the stranger.

"Go back."

The voice was low, harsh, menacing. Almost a croak.

Anthony stopped short. He had to struggle for balance as the plank shuddered under his weight.

"Go back," repeated the voice. "No harm to you, young gentleman. If you go back. But remember – you've seen nobody."

And in some sense, Anthony had not. For under the hat-brim he could see only two eyes regarding him through holes in a black vizard.

Two *Strangers in Vizards*

Even more threatening was the neat grey circle of a pistol muzzle levelled at his chest.

Anthony wavered, empty hands flung out to maintain his balance.

Into his racing mind flashed some dry advice Mandeville had once given him. If the other man has a loaded pistol and you have not, you have only two courses: get very near him, or as far away as possible.

Very near was risky. You needed luck and nerve. True, pistols were unreliable. They often misfired. In which case a deft swordsman would spit his opponent like a chicken – or a strong-armed man would grapple and snatch the weapon. If you did not wish to chance a hero's death, however, and if you had an open line of retreat, it was wiser to back away.

Pistols, Mandeville had added by way of encouragement, were unreliable in another respect: they were hopelessly inaccurate and, except at point-blank range, the odds were against hitting any particular target. They were all right in a cavalry charge fired into a serried mass of pikemen, when you were sure to hit someone. Aimed at a single moving figure, they were not as dangerous as they looked.

"Go back!" repeated the stranger in the mask.

Anthony knew that in this situation he had no choice. If he advanced, the man would blow a hole in his chest, and that would be the end. He could jump to the ground, of course, and draw his rapier – but even if he got it out of its sheath before this fellow shot him, he would be dancing about helplessly, six feet below.

"I'm going," he called back, pretending terrified obedience. The shakiness in his voice was not entirely put on.

Another of Mandeville's warnings came to mind – don't startle anyone who has his weapon trained on you. He's as nervous as you are. But it's his finger, remember, not yours, on the trigger.

Anthony backed a pace or two gingerly, then turned slowly sideways to show he was not planning any surprise movement, and jumped down. "Don't shoot!" he quavered convincingly. He ran across the terrace, as though fleeing obediently the way he had come.

Somehow, though, he must get past the stranger and warn Mandeville – if it was not too late. Every moment was vital. No time to run down to Tobias. He must shout, and hope that Tobias was not too deep in gossip to hear. And his shout might also be heard by Mandeville.

At this range he was probably safe from the pistol. He paused where the path plunged down into the woodland. "Tobias!" he yelled. "Come quick! Help!"

The pistol barked from behind him. He had guessed rightly – the bullet came nowhere near. He wheeled round, sword out of its scabbard. Would the stranger jump down to chase him? No. A shadow flicked back. The arch stood as empty as the tall window-openings that gaped to left and right along the wall.

Pray God that Tobias had heard his shout. He remembered the ear-splitting whistle he had learned to produce as a schoolboy amid the London hubbub. Thrusting two fingertips between his teeth, he sent the sound shrilling down through the treetops. Then, confident that Tobias would now be alerted and listening, he repeated his cry for help. There was an answering yell from below.

Now, without waiting for Tobias, he must get to Mandeville. The wall of the Great Gallery rose like a cliff. Was the masked man still lurking inside the archway or had he gone? He must take a chance. No need, though, to use that way again. The workmen had left ladders leaning against the foot of the wall. Any window would serve.

Ducking in case of further shots, he raced along the terrace, a slanting course, away from the archway, to where a short ladder had been tilted below an end window. Heart in mouth, he twirled it upright against the unfinished sill.

There was no time to think clearly. Afterwards he felt sick, looking back on that moment. It could so easily have been his last. If the stranger had been waiting with his pistol, his brains might have been sprayed upon the morning air.

Just then, though, he had only one idea – an instinct rather, for so it had become since he took service with Mandeville – and that was, at all costs, to join his master. And mercifully there was no one waiting for him when he mounted to the level of the window and peered within.

The unroofed gallery was empty. Immediately opposite, the wall had so far risen only a few courses of stone above the courtyard beyond. Over the top, he caught a fleeting glimpse of running figures. Raised voices, angry and urgent, echoed from the hollow shells of masonry.

He straddled the rough stone sill. The flooring of the gallery would not be laid until the roof was on, so beneath him was a sheer drop of ten feet to where the basement kitchens and larders would one day be. Again, though, the masons had solved his problem. They had left a walkway of planks, dizzily narrow but stout enough to bear their laden barrows, at the height of the future gallery floor.

He clambered through and, steadying himself against the wall on one side, groped along to a broader platform which spanned the building and allowed him to run across into the courtyard.

At once his eye caught Ravenwood's red cloak. Mandeville's less conspicuous figure was beside him. Mandeville had lost his hat. A shaft of early sunshine lit up that familiar head, the dark, red-brown hair flicking above the lace collar as he turned this way and that, defending himself.

There were five – no, six – men attacking the two gentlemen. Mandeville and his lordship could not have survived long but for one advantage. They had posted themselves at the top of a fan-shaped flight of steps, so that their assailants could only come at them from below.

Anthony dashed across the open space, hoping to surprise the enemy. One of them – it was the same russet-coated fellow who had tried to warn him off – stood a few paces behind the others, fumbling to reload his pistol. Another masked man turned and shouted over his shoulder. Out of the medley of furious voices and clashing blades the order rang clear:

"Shoot him, you fool!"

Anthony flew across the unpaved yard. He reached the man with the pistol just as he edged forward to get a clear line of fire between the struggling figures on the steps. Desperation made Anthony murderous. He went for the man's exposed armpit as he levelled his weapon. That, Mandeville had warned him, was a killer's favourite target. A rapier-thrust, at the right angle, would pierce the lung.

He was relieved afterwards that he did not find that angle. His one concern had been to protect his master – at all costs – and he had tried for the most effective hit he knew.

In fact, he missed by inches. But he pinked the man's

upper arm. Howl of pain and crack of pistol sounded together. The stranger reeled away, dropping the firearm and clapping his other hand over the wound. One of his companions swung round, took in the new situation, and came at Anthony with upraised sword.

Anthony braced himself to defend his life.

His own swordsmanship was still rather rough-and-ready. Mandeville had taught him much. Tobias, that lovable but disreputable rascal, had added a few tricks more suited to a back-street brawl than to an affair of honour between gentlemen. The fact remained, he was a craftsman's son, not bred to arms from boyhood. Mandeville and Tobias had drilled him whenever there was opportunity. But fencing did not yet come as an instinct. Wrist and eye and foot did not perfectly co-ordinate.

His opponent was bare-headed. Unkempt black hair, streaked with grey, flopped about the shoulders of a stained leather jerkin. Below the vizard the weathered face was stubbly and unshaven.

The swordplay matched. Here was no gentleman. This was a rough, tough country fighter. But unlike Anthony he had been learning the game for twenty or thirty years.

The wicked blades rasped and slid. The man was of middle height and wiry. In reach and stature they were well paired.

For a full minute they lunged and parried, circling a little, so that Anthony could not see what was happening to Mandeville and Ravenwood. In any case, he had no eyes for anything but the other eyes that gleamed at him through the holes of the vizard. His attention must not stray for an instant.

The blades crossed again. Then, for a split second, they seemed locked. The next thing, Anthony's own rapier was twisted from his fingers by an irresistible force, and sent flashing through the air. The man let out a grunt of triumph.

Anthony sprang back. But the wall was close behind him, and he stood unarmed, unable to escape. The man took a pace towards him, sword levelled for the fatal thrust, but wavering for a few moments undecided.

A voice was heard, the voice Anthony had heard before, telling the man with the pistol to shoot. This time it cried to the swordsman:

"Go on, you dolt! Finish him. I said, 'no witnesses'."

The shout was a death-warrant, but a warrant never executed.

Instinctively, facing that pitiless steel, Anthony closed his eyes. Even if they had been wide open, he would have had no warning of what happened next. Mandeville must have seen his plight and taken a flying leap from the top of the steps. He landed light as a dancer, and the man in the leather jerkin reeled from his assault.

"Quick, lad – up on the steps!"

Curt, urgent, Mandeville tossed the words over his shoulder as he drove back his adversary.

Anthony had enough presence of mind to run and retrieve his own lost weapon. Then, straightening up again, he was in time to face another attacker. They had barely crossed swords when Mandeville swept past him like a human hurricane, clearing their way to the steps.

It was as well. Ravenwood could scarcely have survived much longer. He stood alone at the top, while three of the masked men pressed upwards against him from different angles. The red cloak was bunched round his left arm to give some protection. He swung this way and that, parrying the thrusts, but blood was flowing from his thigh and for all his vigour he was moving painfully.

There was a confused struggle on the shallow, curving steps. Two men turned just in time to face Mandeville's onslaught. One tripped and sprawled headlong. The other gave ground hastily. Anthony, following his master, found himself on the paved platform beside Mandeville and his lordship, glaring down at a little semicircle of panting enemies.

It was still six against three, though several of the strangers were bleeding. But then so was Ravenwood, though he swore under his breath that his wound was nothing.

The man who had fallen was on his feet again, hatless but apparently unhurt. He was a small, nimble man, round-headed and dark. His manner suggested that he was the leader, his clothes indicated the gentleman. When he turned and shouted across the courtyard, his voice was the one Anthony had heard twice before.

"Huw! Davy! Come here!"

From one of the half-finished buildings on the far side came running not two figures but three. The upper half of each face was hidden by a mask of black crape. Each man brandished a sword or dagger.

Anthony's heart turned over within him. Where, in God's name, was Tobias? Hadn't he understood that cry for help? And, if he came now, could Tobias alone make much difference? Certainly the old groom would be of little use, even if his creaky bow-legs could carry him up that steep ascent.

On the spreading fan of the steps, both sides drew breath and eyed each other.

"Who the devil are you?" demanded his lordship. "You will hang for this. I promise you."

The black-haired man laughed unpleasantly. "*I* have promised them something better." He glanced round his party as the new arrivals joined the ring. "Double pay, lads, since there are more than we bargained for. But however many of them, remember – I said no witnesses."

It was at that moment that they all realised there was yet another witness.

Tobias was surveying the scene from a safe distance.

He stood like a black statue, silhouetted against the sunrise blazing through the archway of the Great Gallery. His voice, resonant and challenging, lilted across the expanse of empty ground.

Anthony had no idea what he was shouting. Tobias must be using his native Welsh. Anyhow, the unknown gentleman seemed to understand and was replying in the same language.

The dialogue continued for a minute or two. Tobias sounded indignant and menacing. The old rascal, thought Anthony thankfully, had a natural gift for putting on a false show. Whatever he was saying, it had been enough to make the stranger hesitate before renewing the attack. Tobias had clearly upset his calculations. He wanted no witnesses. And Tobias, standing yonder, out of range and with an open line of escape behind him, would not be easy to eliminate.

Anthony wished there was a similar way of retreat from their own position. But at this stage of the building operations that decorative flight of steps led only to a doorway blocked by a huge stack of bricks.

He looked down at the masked men, a rough bunch if ever he had seen one. He stole a sidelong glance at Mandeville. He could imagine how the quick brain was racing inside that head, questing for some trick to take advantage of this welcome lull. Anthony stood tense, ready to move if he was given his cue. But the ruffians down there were watchful too. Apart from an occasional glance in the direction of Tobias they left the talking to their leader and gave their attention to the three figures at the top of the steps.

Tobias himself must have something in mind. He was clearly playing for time. He went on talking, glib as only Tobias could be. The ringleader of the band beckoned him closer: Tobias was too sensible to put himself in danger – he shook his head vigorously and kept his position of advantage on the raised threshold of the gallery.

The dark gentleman started to walk over towards him, and two men detached themselves from the others, and casually drifted after him: a warning shout from Tobias stopped them in their tracks.

Such a stalemate could not last long. Someone, or something, would be sure to break it. Anthony licked his lips and tightened his grip on his sword-hilt.

What ended the brief lull was a sudden uproar from an unexpected quarter. He heard a babble of excited voices, distant but coming nearer. He stared across to the far right corner of the courtyard, where a gateway led, out of sight, to some other part of the castle.

Tobias had also caught the sound. In English now, and in stentorian tones, he bellowed: "This way, lads! This way!" And round the corner, flooding into view, poured a crowd of homely figures with sticks and shovels.

It was the chance Mandeville must have been waiting for, and Anthony needed no further cue. As the men below instinctively looked round and wavered, Mandeville leapt down upon them. Anthony was barely a moment later.

Even so, he was not quick enough to land another blow. Their attackers were off like hares, racing for the gateway in the corner. It looked as though they would meet the crowd of workmen head-on, but sticks and shovels were no match for cold steel, and the men in the black vizards must have presented an alarming sight. Some of the bolder workmen struck out at them, or tried to grapple with them as they passed, but most were sensible enough to stay clear of those upraised weapons. They fell back to right and left, and the strangers raced through.

It was unfortunate that Mandeville was equally a stranger to the newcomers, and it was his cloak that was grabbed by a brawny young labourer. Mandeville went down. Anthony fell over the pair of them. He leapt to his feet in time to prevent the well-meaning labourer from kneeling on his master's chest.

"Not this gentleman, you fool! This is his lordship's friend!" Massive hands clamped down upon him. His sword was wrested painfully from his hand. Too furious to be frightened of further violence, he burst out: "Let go! Can't you *see*? We have no masks!"

The misunderstanding put right, Mandeville was helped to his feet with apologies, but by this time their real enemies had vanished, pursued through the gateway by an excited pack of men. Mandeville and Anthony hurried after them without much hope. The gateway led into a spacious outer court. A knot of breathless labourers stood leaning on their shovels. Others were trailing back in twos and threes from the gatehouse.

Tobias sheathed his sword. He came towards his master, grinning but apologetic. "Seems they had horses waiting. They're away into the hills by now. No matter, you're all right, both of you."

"A little dazed," said Mandeville mildly.

"You took a knock then, sir?" Tobias looked more anxious.

"No, no. I'm merely bewildered." From Mandeville this was a quite unusual admission. "It was all so quick – and so unexpected. You did well, Tobias. You too, Anthony."

"His lordship not hurt, sir?" said Tobias.

They looked about them. There was no sign of Ravenwood. Mandeville let out a cry of dismay. "He had a wound, yes!" He went rushing back into the inner court, and they hurried after him.

A dozen men were clustered at the foot of the steps. Anthony could see someone stretched on the trampled ground. He saw too the crumpled red cloak. There was no need to ask whose it was.

Three *The Man with No Enemies*

There was a buzz of anger and concern. The weather-beaten faces showed how popular Lord Ravenwood was. A murmur of relief ran round the group as he sat up, and, with a helping hand from two of his men, got shakily to his feet.

"Ah, Renold! Are you all right?" he inquired anxiously. "And that plucky young man of yours?"

"We're both unhurt, Will. You, though?"

"Only my damned leg." His lordship leant heavily on one of the workmen. "That blackguard with the pistol. Soon as I tried to chase after them, over I went."

"Sit down on the steps." Mandeville knelt beside his friend and, after a quick inspection, made a bandage with his sash. "There's no great bleeding now," he said reassuringly. "We must get you home and have the wound properly dressed." He glanced round. "Fetch a hurdle, one of you. Then we can carry his lordship."

"No need for hurdles," said Ravenwood. "Where's my horse?"

Anthony was surprised to see old Thomas at that very moment, riding into the courtyard with his lordship's light bay Spanish gelding. Behind him came workmen leading the other horses.

Tobias stepped forward with Mandeville's hat. He

clutched two others, a rapier and a pistol. His master looked at him with amusement. "You look like a market pedlar."

"Those scoundrels dropped them, sir. If his lordship wants them—" Tobias paused with a dignified air.

"Keep them," begged his lordship. "Spoils of war, eh? You did well for us, Tobias. I shall thank you more properly later." He winced as they lifted him and set him astride his horse. Even so, he did not forget to turn to Anthony with a smile. "You too, Mr Bassey. I'm most obliged." Anthony glowed.

The groom rode off ahead to warn Lady Ravenwood. Mandeville and his lordship followed at a more sedate pace, with Anthony and Tobias at their heels, and an escort of workmen trudging in the rear.

"That was quick action," Anthony murmured. "I was thankful to see you."

"Wasn't no time to dawdle, was it? And when I heard a shot—" Tobias paused significantly.

He had reckoned, he said, that other help might be welcome. So, while he himself had rushed up the path, the old groom had ridden on by the road at full pelt. The road climbed from the river in a long, gently sweeping curve, and reached the main gates of the castle on the far side. Thomas knew that, though there would be no men working on the site this morning, he would find a party busy on a clearance job in the woods near-by. The best thing seemed to be to find them and bring them to the rescue.

Riding through the gates and down this road in the reverse direction, Anthony saw at once how it had just been possible for them to reach the scene in time.

"Only they missed the horses, the clod-hopping clowns," said Tobias disgustedly. "Must have been hidden in those stables – in the outer courtyard – and the dolts rushed past in such a hurry, not one noticed 'em."

"It was more important to get to *us*," said Anthony

27

with feeling.

"Oh, I grant you that, boy. But just two or three could have taken care of those horses. And then, look you, those scoundrels would never have got far! We'd have them all now, laid by the heels. 'Stead of which, where are they?" Tobias flung out his arm in an expressive gesture, taking in the vast horizon that stretched from the Black Mountains to the dim mass of Radnor Forest. "Over the hills and far away."

"That's Wales?" Anthony inquired curiously.

"Wales, England, no matter, boy. Many a man has died in time past, disputing that point. I'm no lawyer to say where county boundaries run. I know the good land is Herefordshire – the English always saw to that. But the mountains, now . . ." He shrugged.

"You shouted to those men in Welsh."

"I thought I'd try them. I reckoned they might pay more heed. And they'd not know what to make of me. Thing was, to win time. Give Thomas a chance to fetch help."

"It worked. If you'd just come running across – as I did – they'd have been too many for us."

Tobias chuckled. "I am no hero. You know me."

"I do know you. If there'd been nothing else to do, you'd have waded into the thick of the fight. You wouldn't have thought twice."

"I thought once, though, didn't I, boy?" Tobias chuckled again.

They were down by the river now, passing the spot where Lord Ravenwood had dismounted and started up the path. The river tumbled noisily behind a fringe of sombre alders, their dull purple catkins contrasting with the silver of the willows. The sun was reaching into the valley bottom. It caught the gleaming white cataracts and the golden drifts of wild daffodils. It was a fair morning, and Anthony could enjoy it now with an oddly relaxed sensation, despite the events of the past half-hour. What was to happen had happened. The day was drained of menace, the tension gone.

They re-crossed the bridge. On the other side the Priory welcomed them back, a friendly place, comforting and comfortable, a higgledy-piggledy pile of ancient, grey monastic buildings, brown brick and pale grey beams and plaster, winking windows and chimneys clustered like organ-pipes.

A white-faced Lady Ravenwood met them at the door, the children goggling from behind her spreading petticoats. His lordship hailed them reassuringly. He was helped tenderly from the saddle and placed in a chair. Eager servants carried him into the house and up the wide staircase to his chamber. Mandeville followed, and Anthony, having no orders to the contrary, followed Mandeville.

There was much fuss now, with the bringing of hot water and clean linen. Ravenwood, his torn and blood-spattered breeches carefully drawn off, lay on his great four-poster, propped up with pillows, and surveyed the damage.

"No break in the bone, by the feel of it," he said with relief.

"And no artery severed," Mandeville declared. "You have not lost too much blood."

"It must be bathed, and bandaged at once," said her ladyship, more herself now that there was something practical to do.

"One moment," said Mandeville. "I fancy the bullet is still in the wound."

"It is," agreed Ravenwood. "And I should know," he added with wry emphasis.

Mandeville peered closer. "It must come out."

Lady Ravenwood was all in a flutter again. "We must send to Hereford. There is a surgeon there—"

"A clumsy old fool," objected her husband. "I would not trust him to butcher a sheep."

"There's no one else. And, Will – the bullet will be *lead*. It must come out, and no time wasted."

"It will take time for a man to ride to Hereford – and to bring back this surgeon, even if he finds him at home . . . It means a day – or longer." Mandeville paused thoughtfully, fingering his beard.

"Oh, Sir Renold!" Lady Ravenwood turned to him in piteous appeal. "Could *you* get it out for him?"

"I think I could," said Mandeville hesitantly, "but I would not fancy the job. And I doubt if poor Will would, either."

"Do your worst – or rather your best." His lordship made a show of cheerfulness. "Give me a cup of wine, and then a thick cloth to bite on. If I cry out then – well, take the children to another part of the house."

"We can do better than that, if you'll trust yourself to my man. Tobias has most delicate fingers. And surprising skill."

"I'll trust your judgement. I think you've had more experience of these things."

"I feel so helpless," said her ladyship. "Time was, a wife knew how to treat her lord's wounds. But in these days no one hereabouts can remember wars and fighting."

A servant was sent to fetch Tobias. Lady Ravenwood hurried off to prepare a drink that would help to dull the pain.

Tobias was ushered in. He came over to the bed, sweeping off his hat and bowing to his noble patient. "If I may wash my hands, my lord?" Water was brought, steaming in the basin. Only when Tobias had scrubbed his hands vigorously did he turn again to Ravenwood, bending his cropped head for a close inspection of the wound. Anthony, hovering helpfully at his elbow, got his first glimpse of the round hole in his lordship's thigh.

Tobias pressed very gently with his finger-tips. "It is not deep, my lord."

"Can you extract it, do you think?"

"I shall do my best." Tobias straightened up. "Here is her ladyship with your posset. If you will drink it first . . ." He stepped back.

"Here, Will," said Lady Ravenwood. She gave him the cup. Anthony caught the fragrance of the hot wine and the spices. "It will give you strength," she said. "There is milk and white of egg beaten in, with rose water and herbs—"

"If I can survive this I can survive anything," said his lordship good-humouredly, but he pressed her hand to show his appreciation. He drank the mixture and gave her the empty cup. "Now, my good fellow," he said in a steady tone. Mandeville, on the far side of the bed, passed him a clean folded towel and he slipped it between his teeth.

Tobias came forward. Suddenly, as though from nowhere, a knife appeared in his hand. Lady Ravenwood let out a little scream. "Must you cut him?"

"It will be nothing, my lady."

Tobias leant forward. With a deft, decisive movement he drew a line from left to right across the flesh. Then, with a turn of the wrist, a second line. With an awful fascination Anthony saw fresh blood well up through the incisions, making a vivid red cross on Ravenwood's thigh, with the bullet-hole at the centre.

"Hold this," Tobias grunted, passing him the knife. "Careful, boy – it's razor sharp." Anthony took it gingerly.

Tobias put both hands on the wound, squeezing the flesh. On his left thumb the old branded letter T stood out lividly against the healthy colour of the surrounding skin. Anthony remembered his own shock when he had first seen that hangman's mark. He wondered if Lord Ravenwood had noticed, and how he felt about entrusting himself to a man who had once so narrowly escaped hanging at Tyburn. But his lordship had other things to feel, and more acutely. He twitched under the Welsh-man's touch and the faintest sound came from the muff-ling towel. His eyes were closed.

"There," said Tobias suddenly. "Popped out like a cherry-stone!"

He stood up, triumphantly displaying between blood-smeared finger and thumb the wicked little ball that had done the damage. There was a general gasp of relief around the bed. Ravenwood opened his eyes, tossed aside his gag, and cried delightedly: "You've done it? You have light fingers indeed, Tobias!"

"That opinion has been expressed before," said Mandeville with a sly twinkle in his eye. He caught Anthony's glance and added gravely, "Indeed, by one of the best judges in the kingdom." In the chorus of grati-tude and congratulation nobody else seemed to detect the irony.

"It is a clean wound, my lord," said Tobias, who was vastly enjoying his popularity. "If it is dressed now it should heal quickly. Your lordship is young and healthy. You will soon be in the saddle once more."

At that moment, however, his lordship felt much more inclined to sink back on his pillows and sleep, which was hardly surprising after the soothing concoc-tion he had just swallowed. His last waking thought was for his guests – they had had no breakfast yet and it was near dinner-time. So, the wound bathed and ban-daged, and the patient settled in drowsy comfort, every-one withdrew except his personal servant, Robert, who remained to watch over him.

Anthony became suddenly aware that he was faint with hunger, and he was more than willing when their hostess invited him, with Mandeville, to tell her the full story over dinner in the family's private apartments.

Now, for the first time, he heard Mandeville's account. He had been walking round the courtyard with his lordship, who was expounding the main plan and inviting suggestions for the final decorative details. A faint, distant sound – Anthony's first shout – had stopped him in his tracks. Ravenwood had heard nothing and, being intent upon his cherished designs, had impatiently dismissed it as mere fancy. The pistol-shot had changed his opinion. When masked men had rushed from their hiding-place they had missed all hope of a surprise attack from the rear, and the two friends had been able to reach the vantage-point of the steps.

Anthony told his own story.

"So," said Mandeville. "Someone was watching us when we came along beside the river." He turned to her ladyship. "Will goes that way every morning?"

"Unless the weather is foul. Both for the exercise and to see the progress of the building. If there are men working, he talks to them. At other times, he likes to prowl about by himself – and check that it is all well done, without offence to any of them." She smiled affectionately. "And I believe he loves just to walk there and dream. The new castle has become a great thing with him."

"So I can see."

"Lately, he's become even more impatient to get it finished."

"Has the project caused any unpleasantness?"

Her eyes widened. "Unpleasantness? How could it? The work has put money in everyone's pocket. Everyone is delighted." She laughed softly. "I think I am the only one with any doubts about the move – but even I hadn't thought of resorting to a pistol! It is what he wants, and I only want him to be happy."

"There's been no workman dismissed? No quarrel with architects or contractors?"

She shook her head. "You know Will. No one is more generous. He and the architect are like brothers. Everybody – *everybody* – is with them in this project."

Mandeville was silent for a few moments. He took a

drink of wine and dabbed his beard. "It is rather a con-
undrum, then. This was a carefully planned attack by
someone who knew his daily habits. Can you think of
anything else he can have done to stir up enmity? A great
landlord like Will – with all his estates and tenants and
work-people—"

"They all love him," said Lady Ravenwood stoutly.
"I would swear, Will has not an enemy in the world."

Mandeville bowed his head in courteous agreement.
Anthony was glad that he did not continue his questioning, for he could see that their hostess was getting a little
warm with indignation. She rose now, and they stood
up respectfully. She must return to my lord's chamber
and see how he was.

Mandeville smiled at Anthony across the table. "Not
an enemy in the world?" he repeated doubtfully, when
the door had closed behind her. "I think a man who
never made an enemy never made anything of great consequence."

Four *Wildhope*

Sitting up in his ornate four-poster that evening, a much recovered Lord Ravenwood chewed a roast chicken leg and discussed the mysterious events of the morning.

"No notion *who* they were," he said. "Couldn't even recognise the fellow who led them. And my steward has been all round the estate people who came and helped us. No one could identify any of them. Or their horses."

"Nine men," said Mandeville thoughtfully. "Armed, masked, with horses hidden, ready saddled... A very carefully prepared ambush. It must have been for you, not me."

"Of course it was for me, my dear Renold! I go up there most mornings. And usually alone. No one knew you were even coming to Crucorney – didn't myself till you rode up to the door yesterday, and very delighted I was."

"I have got into the habit of not announcing my plans – it's unfair to my friends, but my way of life is rather different—"

"Mad Mandeville, eh? I know."

"I do have my enemies – Rose says *you* have not. There are people in this country and abroad who would cheerfully have me knocked on the head. But, as you say, they could not have planned to find me there."

"No, no, they were after me. Perhaps a gang of robbers – this is a lawless corner of the kingdom. They'd know I'd have rings – my rapier would be worth something – there are jewels on my pocket-watch. I've no doubt those scoundrels would have stripped me to the skin."

"H'm." Mandeville did not sound satisfied. "Your wealth is famous. Even so, between nine men . . . and why didn't they make off when they met with such resistance?"

"They stood their ground, I grant you. For men of that sort they were most extraordinarily determined."

"They meant to kill."

Anthony ventured a word himself. "The one who led them – he kept saying 'no witnesses'."

"So he did, Mr Bassey!"

"And he said something about 'double pay' – "

"It doesn't sound like a gang of common thieves," said Mandeville. "More like men hired to murder you."

"That makes no sense, no sense at all. My death would be of no benefit to anyone. I have injured nobody. I've done nothing to make anyone seek revenge. Rose is right. I have no enemies."

They could not budge his lordship from that conviction. So the next morning they rode on their way, leaving their host comfortable in his bed and the enigma no nearer solution.

They took a solitary road, one of the broad green drove roads by which, in autumn, the cattle from Wales and these border counties started their long doomed march to Smithfield market in London. It was another fine morning, with clear views to the high western horizon where lingering snow still dappled the hills. They kept an eye open for trouble, but were hardly surprised to meet none. If a second attempt were made it would be against Lord Ravenwood, not themselves, and he for the time being was safe in the Priory, with plenty of his own men to protect him.

Anthony's thoughts turned to their destination. All his service with Mandeville had been spent either at the shabby lodgings off Fleet Street or in sundry travelling at home and abroad. He was curious to set eyes, for the first time, on the young baronet's country home.

Wildhope Hall was a name with a most fitting ring to it, matching Mandeville's temperament and restless way of life. In fact, though, as Mandeville had explained to him, "hope" was only a common word in these parts for a small enclosed valley. The "wild" similarly referred to the lack of cultivation, and now no longer applied. Many generations of energetic Mandevilles had changed all that.

"And if they hadn't," he chuckled, "my lady mother would."

Anthony was even more curious to see her. It was odd, somehow, to think of Mandeville with a mother. Or to imagine Mandeville ever as a boy, obedient to parents, compelled to explain himself and answer for his movements. Yet it could not have been so many years ago. He and Lord Ravenwood were much of an age, and, though his lordship had a wife and two small children, he had married young.

Lady Mandeville sounded a formidable woman. "She's a terror, boy," Tobias had said darkly. "You'll see."

She had taken over more and more the running of the estate during the last years of her husband's life. When death claimed him after his lengthy illness, Mandeville had inherited the title and land but had not had the heart to rob his mother of the position she enjoyed. So, until such time as he found a wife and brought her home, Lady Mandeville remained mistress of Wildhope and managed the estate for him.

It was seldom indeed that he made the long journey home. Yet this morning, as he reined in on the crest of Pendock Hill and pointed downwards, there was an unusual softness in his voice.

"There we are. The house where I was born."

After the rambling, old-fashioned opulence of the Priory, Wildhope Hall looked a modest residence, tall but compact, a huddle of steep gables crowning walls of mellow brickwork and moulded plaster in an elaborate frame of oaken beams, with tiny window-panes flashing back the golden light of noon. It nestled amid orchards and gardens, with long ranges of barns and stables to north and east. A pool gleamed, a rivulet wound like a bright ribbon between the green velvet of the lower meadows. The air was loud with the bleating of lambs and the lowing of cattle.

They must have been sighted riding down the hill. As they swung out of their saddles in the yard, Lady Mandeville greeted her son briskly from the doorway.

"At last! I looked for you a week ago."

"I'm sorry, Mother, I had things to do in town."

He ran up the steps and flung his arms round her. There was no lack of warmth in their greeting, Anthony noticed.

She freed herself, stepped back, and inspected him. She was smaller than Anthony had pictured her – like a plump little bird, and with sharp darting eyes to match. Nor was she dressed like a grand lady. Her drab skirts were looped up to keep the hem off the ground, but not with complete success for they were spattered with dry mud. She wore an apron and would have passed in any market as a farmer's wife.

"You still want flesh on your bones," she accused Mandeville.

"I lead an active life, Mother. And you're not purposing to send me up to Smithfield?"

"Pert as ever!" But she laughed, taking his retort in good part. "If I had my way you would not see London again, never mind Smithfield." She turned and stared at Anthony, eyeing him up and down as he stood there, turning his hat-brim in his hand. "I suppose this is your Italian youth?"

"This is Anthony Bassey. His father indeed came from Venice, but his mother is as English as you are. Mr Bassey now serves me as my secretary." Anthony noted gratefully the emphasis, faint but unmistakable, laid upon the "Mister".

Lady Mandeville ignored it. "Secretary? Ho, ho! When did *you* ever send any letters? I cannot get you to sign the documents needed for the conduct of your estate. Well, perhaps we shall see an improvement now." She addressed herself to Anthony, fixing him with a disapproving eye. "You can write English?" she demanded doubtfully.

"Yes, my lady."

Mandeville laughed a little impatiently. "He was born in London, Mother. He went to school at St Paul's. He learned French also and Latin – he can help you with those old legal documents – and of course his father has taught him Italian."

"H'm. We have little call for Italian in Herefordshire. As for lawyers' Latin, I can piece out their rigmarole well enough for myself." She wheeled on her son with a challenging look. "Do you ever recall my being worsted in a case over leases or land boundaries or anything else?"

"I do not, dear Mother. You are not one to be beaten."

"And well for you and the estate that I'm not!" Her gaze roved across the little courtyard. A groom was leading Mandeville's mare to the stables, and Tobias followed with his own mount and Anthony's. "You have brought that rogue Fludd, I see."

"Tobias? Naturally."

"Well, it's your house, you must bring whom you please. But I'd sleep sounder without a convicted thief under our roof."

"Now, Mother!" Mandeville kept his tone light, but Anthony saw the vexed flush on the high cheekbones.

"That is an old story. Tobias is a reformed sinner. Anyhow, we're the last people he'd steal from. You forget – I saved his neck."

"I can't think why."

"Oh, the lilt of his voice amid all that London babble in the court. It carried me straight back to the Marches of Wales. You mayn't believe it, but I *can* be homesick."

"Then you should come home more often," she said tartly. Then her manner softened. "We mustn't start our bickering before you've crossed the threshold. You'll be hungry, and the clock's upright." She gestured towards the dial high on the stable-wall, and Anthony, foxed for a moment by the unfamiliar country phrase, saw that the gilded hand was pointing up at twelve. "Dinner-time!" And with her son's arm curved affectionately round her shoulders she led the way indoors.

Anthony followed at a respectful distance. After this long separation they would want to be alone. They must have so much to say.

Lady Mandeville certainly had. But Anthony quickly realised that her son was disinclined to answer all her eager questions. Anthony was bidden to join them at the table in a small panelled chamber upstairs above the gateway. His presence was to be used to provide some check, at least, on her ladyship's outspoken tongue.

"And how did you leave young Will?" she asked, pouring tawny cider into their pewter tankards. "Is his wound grave?"

"Ah, you heard of that little business?"

"Of course I heard. We hear the news. Even without newsletters!" She seized a knife and began to carve generous slices from a leg of fragrantly steaming roast mutton. "And as soon as I heard, I guessed my crazy son would be mixed up in it."

"I wasn't scratched. Will was shot in the leg, but it's a clean wound, healing well, and already he's itching to go limping round his new buildings. But it might have gone differently if it hadn't been for Tobias – and Anthony here." Mandeville gave his mother a searching look. "I know how the news travels through the countryside. Tell me, have you heard any whisper about who it could have been?"

She shook her head. "No, Renold. We are all amazed that anyone should do such a thing. Some unknown horsemen were seen later that morning, but from far off. They were taken for a hunting party, and nothing thought of it till afterwards. Has Ravenwood no notion?"

"None at all. So – if you hear more – and I know that few matters escape my dear mother's sharp ear in this part of the kingdom—"

"I would tell you at once," she promised. "And if you were not here I would send word to Ravenwood himself. I have a high regard for that young man. Though he is squandering impossible sums upon this unnecessary new castle of his!"

"He can afford it."

"I know. But extravagance is something I cannot abide." She turned to Anthony and, with a friendlier look than she had given him before, pressed him to carve himself more mutton. Anthony accepted gladly. He was ravenous from his morning ride, and he had never tasted such delicious meat. Lady Mandeville might disapprove of extravagance but she kept a lavish table.

Anthony was quiet while the others talked. Lady Mandeville asked after the family at Crucorney. To her, Anthony noted, they were just neighbours, good neighbours, but no better in blood than the Mandevilles. Ravenwood might be a lord while her son was a mere baronet. He might own twenty times as much land, with all his estates in other counties, and have fifty times the income. But neither he nor his father before him had ever patronised the Mandevilles. She was pleased to hear that, just as Will and Renold had played as children, so as grown men they met as equals still.

"He is my notion of a true gentleman," she said.

"But has he made enemies?"

She shook her head decisively. "No. As for provoking an outrageous attack like this... Time was, I know, when there was little law in these border counties, families had feuds. Disputes were settled in rougher ways then. But all that is lost in antiquity now."

The Ravenwoods had always been well regarded, Will's father just as much as Will. The lord before that – Will's uncle – had perhaps been less liked by some, being a reserved man, a solemn bachelor, who had turned back to the old religion.

"But, bless my soul, he was no worse for that! He was not the only Papist hereabouts – some of the best families were. They were loyal though, they kept the law, they paid their fines for not attending parish church, and it was their own business what prayers they said in their own houses. Will's uncle was as much respected as any of them. Still," Lady Mandeville admitted, "it was a happy day when Will's father succeeded to the title, and there was a lady again at the Priory, and children born there." She signed to Anthony to cut himself some apple pie, then looked hard at Mandeville. "That pretty Susanna, Will's younger sister. What a match we could have arranged there! If you had given me the chance."

"She has done much better, Mother, marrying a viscount."

"You could have had her. Mandeville blood is good enough for anyone. And with the dowry she would have brought you, joined to Wildhope—"

"I am sorry, Mother. I have told you before. I shall never marry just to enlarge the estate."

Lady Mandeville was not to be put down. She merely changed her tack.

"Will has a daughter. *She* must be nearly eight."

"I have no idea. Margaret is a charming child—"

"You noticed that?" said Lady Mandeville hopefully.

"But far too young to fit into your deep-laid schemes."

"Why, Renold? Many an heiress is betrothed at her age. She could be wedded at twelve – stay at home then with her mother, of course, until she was ready for married life – but the legal documents would all have been signed—"

"And that of course is the main thing?" Mandeville's face darkened with anger. "It hardly seems to me an ideal arrangement."

"Not ideal, no. I would sooner see you married now to some suitable wife, and then children coming—"

Mandeville's stool scraped back from the table as he jumped to his feet. "Must we always have this when I come?"

Lady Mandeville looked up at him without blenching. "Until you face your responsibilities. You go roving about the world – and I have some notion what dangers you get into, little though you tell me. You could have been killed the other morning, even at Crucorney. What would have happened then to Wildhope?"

"You would have gone on running the place as you always have."

"I shall not live for ever, Renold. You must have an heir, it's your duty—"

"I *have* an heir. My beloved sister. If anything happens to me before I have a child myself, Wildhope can go to Priscilla – and her brood after her—"

"Priscilla could not inherit the title—"

"Devil take the title, then. I shall marry – if I do – when I'm so minded. And it will be for love, not land."

Mandeville swept out of the room.

Anthony finished his meal in an awkward silence. Only once did Lady Mandeville address a remark to him. Turning with a taut-lipped smile she said, "I do my best, Mr Bassey. I have broken horses in my time. I shall not let my own son defeat me."

Then, and even more in the next two or three days, Anthony understood why Mandeville chose his way of life, whether in a cheap London lodging or travelling in far-off places.

There was no doubt that he loved Wildhope. There were moments, especially early in the day, alone in the great bed-chamber which his mother insisted on keeping for his use, when Anthony could hear him singing as he dressed. His eyes brightened as he walked round with Anthony, pointing out the favourite places he remembered from his childhood, telling absurd stories of what had happened here or there. He was welcomed warmly by everyone they encountered, and he was warm in return, except when questioned too closely on his future plans.

Nor was there any doubt of the love between him and his mother. Only, Anthony saw, they were like flint and steel. They could not be long together without sparks flying.

Lady Mandeville's whole world was this corner of the Marches, especially the family estate. She sniffed at a reference to France or Italy. It was fifteen years since she had been to London – the old-fashioned cut of her gown, when she dressed more elegantly in their honour in the evenings, was evidence of that.

"And I have no wish to see London again," she said. "Or for that matter to cross the Severn!"

They had an hour or two to themselves after breakfast, while she ordered the household affairs. Then she was ready to ride out, sitting very upright on her stocky hill pony, and her son must accompany her, to show his face to the tenants and see what had been done in his name since his last visit.

"Mr Bassey had better come too. And you, young

man," she said severely, "had better take some notes."

"Notes, my lady?"

"Notes. Sir Renold has a poor memory for what I tell him. So, when I am forced to write to him in London – or some other God-forsaken place – it would help if he knew what I was talking about, so that he could send me a decision. I shall look to you, Mr Bassey. See that my letters are promptly answered, and that the answers are not solely demands for more money!"

"I will do my best, my lady."

They rode for miles each morning and afternoon, up or down that secluded valley, and over the rounded flanks of the hills to seek out even remoter farms. Tenants came hurrying across the fields at their approach, doffing their hats and breaking into smiles as Mandeville gave them a greeting. Then, as his mother took over the conversation, keeping it firmly to practical matters, Anthony saw his eyes glaze and his attention wander.

Anthony, striving to make a note or two as directed, found it hard to make out the speech of these west countryfolk, and Lady Mandeville was little easier to understand as she dropped more and more into the same idiom.

"Of course you can pay your rent, Fletcher! I know what a good haul-in you had last season."

Or, briskly, "I'm sorry your wife's been feeling kecky. I'll send her a sovereign remedy of my own. But tell her from me, work is the best medicine."

Or, "As we came by, I saw your bottom lezzar was still quobby. When are you going to stir your stumps and dig that ditch?" She turned to Anthony, saw his mystified look, and impatiently translated: "Hunt's lower meadow is water-logged. He has promised to drain it." And again: "Chimmock, Mr Bassey? *Chimney*, if you prefer – I shall send my mason to repair the chimney. I understood from Sir Renold that you had a full command of English!"

One evening there had to be an endless candle-lit session over the rent-roll and the estate accounts. Lady Mandeville strewed the supper table with ledgers and receipts, tally-sticks, letters and lists, with crumpled old parchment leases and title-deeds handy for reference.

The steward, a silent, hatchet-faced man named Woodward, was in attendance, and Anthony had to draw up a stool beside his master and do his best to follow the wearisome discussions. Each ended in much the same way, with Mandeville murmuring impatiently, "Whatever you say, dear Mother. I leave it to you and Woodward to decide."

Anthony wondered how long this Herefordshire visit would continue. He knew better than to ask. But Tobias said, with a dark chuckle, "I give it another three days. Not more."

It was Tobias, as it turned out, who brought their stay to an end.

Anthony had noticed him polishing the pistol and rapier dropped by the masked marauders in their flight. Tobias, one might be sure, would get the best price for them when they got back to London. One of the hats, too, he admitted, the one worn by the leader of the party, was beaver of good quality, and, when furbished up, would be very marketable. The other, worn and greasy, was fit only for a November guy.

Later that evening, when Tobias lighted their way upstairs he lingered in Mandeville's room.

"I've come upon something, sir, I think you ought to see."

He handed his master a small oblong of much-folded paper.

"Another paper I ought to see?" said Mandeville with a good-humoured groan. He had heard that phrase from his mother a dozen times in the last few days. But his expression changed when he had taken it to the light to read. "Where did you find this, Tobias?"

"I was cleaning up a hat – that gentleman's hat I picked up at Crucorney. The letter was tight folded, just like that, inside the hatband."

Five *Motives for Murder?*

Mandeville called to Anthony, who was standing in the doorway between their rooms. "What do you make of this?"

Anthony went over and inspected the grubby sheet of paper. The handwriting was careless, with bold flourishes. He read:

> *Sir, Your answer was brought me last night at Windsor, and I am glad we are of the same mind and can be of service to each other. How the business is to be accomplished I leave to you. Your second plan commends itself most to me – if our friend were discovered with his neck broken, fallen from one of these fine new buildings he is setting up, that would be best, for it would appear an accident. But what matters is that it be accomplished one way or another, so long as there be no witnesses and no tracing of it back to you – and me. As to that last, do not write to me again, for there is no need to take the risk. I shall know swiftly if you have succeeded. The sudden death of any nobleman is always talked of at court. You have my word then that all your debts will be settled, according to the list you furnished me. You know the sole condition – if you allow, by carelessness, the least breath of suspicion to blow upon my name, you will make it impossible for me to pay a penny. And so, good fortune in your enterprise.*

Anthony turned over the letter. There was no name or superscription of any sort.

"And no signature," said Mandeville. "It would be surprising if there were – for one who writes such a flamboyant hand, the sender is singularly modest about his identity." He refolded the paper, so that the broken sealing-wax edges came together. No pattern was traceable. "He used his thumb. He would not even risk his signet-ring."

"No need, sir. The man who received this would know who sent it."

"I fancy he might still have preferred a signature," said Mandeville dryly. "I know I should."

"But he couldn't insist, sir! The man writing mentions 'court' and 'Windsor' – he's a person of rank. If the letter was sent to the man who led the attack on Lord Ravenwood—"

"Well, it was in his hat. Where he mistakenly thought it would be safe."

"That man might pass for a gentleman – of a sort. But a rough country gentleman. Not a courtier, not one of the great ones. I think he'd have to take the other man's word that he'd keep his promise."

"Good reasoning. Perhaps my mother can shed some light on this in the morning."

Next day, as soon as he was dressed, Mandeville hurried off to his mother's chamber. But that energetic lady was already downstairs. Anthony caught up with them both in the parlour, where she was standing at the table, breaking her fast on a buttered crust and a tankard of small ale.

"A gentleman in these parts who is burdened with his debts?" She echoed her son's question sardonically. "I could name you a dozen."

"But one who would commit a murder to get them paid?"

"Ah, that narrows the field. Be good enough to come in, Mr Bassey, and close that door behind you."

"A smallish man," went on Mandeville, "about forty

years old. Dark, with a round head – large for his height, to judge by the size of his hat.''

''And knowing Welsh, you said before?''

''He called to his men in Welsh – and to Tobias.''

Lady Mandeville pursed her lips. ''One name suggests itself. Sir Dudley Ruthin. A wild fellow by repute. The Ruthins are all wild. Violent and quarrelsome. They live as their forefathers lived in the bad old days. It is not surprising they have not prospered.'' She considered. ''Your description fits, though I haven't clapped eyes on Sir Dudley these ten years. We are scarcely neighbours, I am thankful to say. The Ruthin lands – such as they are – lie miles away. North of here.'' A thought struck her. ''Those horsemen who were seen that day. They could well have been Sir Dudley and his party on their way home.''

''Thank you, Mother. I must take this letter to Crucorney.'' He filled a tankard, took a slice of bread, and motioned Anthony to help himself. ''Will may want my help. I can't say when I shall be back.''

''I can. I know you, Renold. You're off again. But not before you have signed the last of those documents.''

Anthony was thankful to slip away and see to their simple packing. Tobias, he found, had already ordered their horses.

Soon they were riding back along the old drove road. It was a slate-grey morning, and gusty showers whipped their cheeks. Mandeville spoke little, and set a smartish pace. ''His lordship has two enemies, never mind one,'' he said grimly. ''He needs to be told.'' He rode on in silence, and Anthony was glad of his master's sense of urgency.

That letter had an ugly ring. Again he felt menace in the air, as he had done on that other morning.

Nervously he scanned the landscape. Was it as empty as it looked? It stretched right and left, a day's journey in either direction, from the undulating spine of the steep

Malverns in the east, like some crouched monster, to the long straight horizon of the Black Mountains, breaking sharply to fall into the valley of the Wye. Today it was a leaden landscape, except for the arch of the heavens, and that had a sullen brazen light, diffused from the over-clouded sun.

But of course no one appeared ᵕ bar their passage. The sinister quality of the day was all in his fancy. Before noon they were dismounting at Crucorney Priory.

His lordship welcomed them in his bedchamber, sitting at a bright coal fire with his leg stuck out before him on a footstool and a favourite old hound, Bellman, sprawled beside his chair. The air was blue with pipe-smoke. He had books around him, Gervase Markham's *Discourse of Horsemanship* and Henry Wotton's *Elements of Architecture* and Shakespeare's plays, from which he was reading to his children the fairy scenes from *A Midsummer Night's Dream*. He was restless and eager for adult company. Margaret and little Gilbert were sent off, to their obvious disappointment, to say that Sir Renold and Mr Bassey would be taking dinner with him in his room.

As soon as they had scampered away, Mandeville pulled out the letter. Ravenwood scanned it thoughtfully. Mandeville put forward his mother's suggestion.

"Ruthin?" Ravenwood repeated the name. "Wait . . . I recall something. But long ago – in my grandfather's time. A lawsuit over some land in South Wales."

"Did your grandfather win the case?"

"Yes – fortunately as it turned out. There's coal there. We do very well out of it." He pointed to the writhing flames in the grate. "And the income from those pits is helping to build the castle."

Anthony could imagine that the present Ruthin was less pleased.

"How long ago was this?" asked Mandeville. He had

drawn up another chair. Anthony, at a nod and a smile from Ravenwood, found himself a stool.

"It was 1588," said Ravenwood with surprising exactness. "Armada year. My father once told me the Ruthins hated our family far more than ever they hated the Spaniards."

"A long time to bear a grudge," said Mandeville, "but my mother tells me they live in the past. The old sort of border people, quarrelsome as cats, carrying on feuds from generation to generation. Have you ever met Sir Dudley?"

Ravenwood shook his head. "No. You remember the junketing my father put on to celebrate my coming-of-age?"

"Who could forget it? Everyone came from miles and miles."

"Not the Ruthins. Father invited them. It seemed only civil." Ravenwood smiled ruefully. "He got a mighty uncivil answer."

"So, even if it *was* Sir Dudley the other morning—"

"I shouldn't have recognised him, with or without a mask."

They were interrupted by the entry of three servants in procession, carrying silver-covered dishes. One of the new-fangled gate-leg tables was brought forward and its curved flaps raised. Anthony noted, with pleasant expectation, a joint of roast veal and a dish of hot salmon, with ox tongue, ham, cheese and a tansy pudding to provide for any unfilled corners.

"Mr Bassey will carve for us," said his lordship. Having set out the wine-glasses, platters and other necessaries, the men bowed and silently withdrew.

Mandeville was eager to get back to their discussion. "Have you sent a report to the Lord Lieutenant?"

"No. Nor shall I."

Mandeville raised his eyebrows. "Surely – this was an armed affray. He's responsible for keeping the King's peace in this county."

"What can he do? I can't name Ruthin. And it won't stop at the Lord Lieutenant – the Privy Council will hear of it – it will do me no good at court. I'll be talked of as some undependable fellow who gets involved in lawless broils — "

Ravenwood shifted uncomfortably in his crimson velvet chair. Anthony wondered suddenly, was his lordship's unease due to the pain of his wound or to some secret embarrassment? Had Ravenwood more understanding of this letter than he was prepared to admit?

Mandeville, Anthony observed, was studying his old friend with a sharply sceptical eye. "Since when did *you* care about your reputation at court?" he inquired. "How many years is it since you showed your face there?"

"This may surprise you," said Ravenwood. "I paid my respects to His Majesty last summer, when he was on progress in Oxfordshire. And in the autumn I was at Richmond, and again in London, at Whitehall."

"It does not surprise me as much as you think," Mandeville answered softly.

"Had you heard, then?"

"No. But this letter shows you have a second enemy – perhaps a more dangerous one. Certainly more powerful. Obviously a courtier. Therefore, I suspect you have been to court yourself."

"And I shall again, as soon as this confounded leg is healed," said Ravenwood defiantly.

"The devil you will! Why? Don't tell me you're going in quest of royal favour – you, of all people?"

Anthony could understand Mandeville's amazement. In his own brief acquaintance with Ravenwood he had summed up his lordship as a great country gentleman, wrapped up in horses and dogs and sports of many kinds, full of projects for building and laying out new gardens and in every way perfecting this already lovely corner of his native Herefordshire.

Ravenwood struck him as a straightforward, almost simple, character, the very last person to join the pack of fawning hypocrites competing for the favour of King Charles.

Ravenwood had flushed slightly. "Don't misunderstand me, Renold. It's high time some honest men did 'go in quest of royal favour', as you put it. Or this country will soon be in a worse state than it already is."

"But – Will! I can't see you amid the intrigues of Whitehall. You'd hate it."

"I probably shall. But one must sometimes put up with unpleasant things – or nothing worth while gets done."

Mandeville's eyes narrowed. "You've changed, Will," he said. "What's happened to change you?"

"What I saw at court." Diffidently, almost apologetically, Ravenwood enlarged upon the matter. "I was surprised – no, I was frankly appalled – to see the sort of men who surround His Majesty."

Mandeville nodded. "You would be."

"But, Renold, these are the men he *listens* to!" Ravenwood's voice was alive with anxiety. "He meets few others."

"His Majesty is a very shy man. A very good man, but painfully reserved. It is often said," Mandeville added quietly, "that the King is devoted to his people – but he dislikes meeting them."

"But that's bad! Don't you see how bad it is? What would my estates be like if I weren't prepared to ride round them continually – if I didn't talk to tenants and bailiffs, yes, ploughmen and shepherds, anyone who wants a word with me? It's the only way to do it."

"My mother would agree with you," said Mandeville with a smile. "But England and Wales – not to mention Scotland and Ireland – add up to rather more than an estate. Even estates as large as yours."

"I know, I know. The King can't be everywhere – he can't do everything himself. I'm not a complete fool. He must have help, but – God save us! – what help has he? He hasn't called a Parliament for years. Even I, a peer of the realm, have no place where I can meet my fellows and hear what they think. We have no House of Commons – yet the kingdom is full of sound country gentlemen, lawyers, level-headed men of business, city merchants, travelled men who know the world. Who asks *their* opinion? And from lack of common sense and experience the affairs of the nation drift from bad to worse! Trade, taxes, everything."

Anthony listened with ever-quickening interest. He had not expected to hear such views from a great lord like Ravenwood.

Himself, growing up in the quick-witted, free-speaking atmosphere of the city, he was accustomed from childhood to blunt criticisms of the court. In London men spoke their minds. From rich aldermen down to market porters, from the preachers in St Paul's to the precocious schoolboys disputing in their debates, there was constant grumbling about the state of the country. He had not realised, though, that there were noblemen who felt the same.

In his own case his judgement had been further sharpened by having an Italian father. Coming from a strictly constituted republic like Venice, Pietro Bassi still viewed the slipshod English ways with a cynical, incredulous eye. England had given him freedom of one kind, to practise his skill as a glassworker for better pay than he could have earned at home. But in many other ways, he had privately confessed to Anthony, he was amazed that the free English put up with the arbitrary government of these Scottish Stuart kings.

As though suddenly aware that he had another listener besides his boyhood friend, Ravenwood turned and addressed Anthony.

"Now don't misunderstand me, young fellow—"

"Of course, not, my lord."

"I yield to nobody in loyalty to His Majesty—"

"I'd never think otherwise, my lord."

"Good." Ravenwood grinned amiably. "Don't want you running off with garbled stories to the Privy Council! I mean to keep my head on my shoulders – and my ears stuck to it still. The King, God bless him, is a fine man. But in practice he lets the country be run by a little group, a cabinet of inner councillors, getting together on Sunday mornings after service – and settling everything to suit themselves. I am damned if I see why."

"You will be damned if you say so too openly," said Mandeville.

"I shall say it, none the less. I've seen these men," went on his lordship explosively. "Cottington – no moral scruples, none whatever. Pembroke – overbearing, blasphemous buffoon, not merely illiterate, positively boasts of it! Young Lennox – a good-natured simpleton – looks like a horse, which is very well for a horse to look, but not a duke! Coke, Windebanke, Harry Vane – now *he's* well named – self-important little peacock—"

"You must have enjoyed yourself at court. But be fair," said Mandeville more seriously, "they are not all fools and rogues."

"I grant you that. There are some good men too. But even they, Renold – they're too *limited*. They're shut up in this close court atmosphere, they don't know what ordinary men are thinking and feeling up and down the country, they need to go out and about more—"

"Perhaps they daren't."

Ravenwood stared at him across the table. "Daren't? No one would harm them."

"Daren't turn their backs on their fellow courtiers, I mean. If you're at the centre of things, it's best to stay

there. Don't take your eye off your rivals. Otherwise –
go away for a month, come back – you'll have a nasty
surprise." Mandeville changed tack. "How did you get
on with the King?"

"Excellently."

"What did you talk about?"

"At our first meeting, it was only about horses. His
Majesty is very knowledgeable."

"That was good – you had an interest in common."

"It seemed so. I found the King most cordial—"

"You were lucky. He's not a talkative man. You
might take him for a cold fish, but you'd be wrong. It's
his painful shyness – and his stammer – and this determination to keep up the royal dignity. Makes it hard for
him to form friendships."

"He was friendly to me. If he had not been – if he had
not positively encouraged me – I would not have presented myself at court again."

"But you did," said Mandeville thoughtfully. "At
Richmond, and then at Whitehall. To talk about
horses?"

"Not all the time!" Ravenwood stopped, seeing that
he was being teased. "But you must watch for your
moment with the King. If you want to change the
subject, you have to do it rather discreetly."

"You're learning, Will! You'll make a courtier yet."

"I mean to." In his lordship's quiet tone there was determination. "There must be a change in the men
who're round the King. And, Renold, this is not just
some notion of my own – I've had encouragement, from
more than one quarter. I think I'm needed, they say
there's room for a man like me—"

"'They say'? So, I take it, you've not kept your opinions altogether secret?"

"You know me. I speak my mind, wherever I am."

Naturally, thought Anthony. Except in the King's
own presence, a man of his lordship's rank had never in

his life needed to guard his tongue. Lucky Ravenwood.

Mandeville smiled sadly. "Yet you can't believe that you've already made yourself one powerful enemy at court? Someone who is determined that you are far too dangerous to let into the charmed circle at Whitehall? And who thinks it would be simplest to eliminate you now?"

"I can't believe it. Intrigue, yes – slanders. But *murder*?"

"Did we dream the other morning? The bullet in your leg? And now this letter I brought you today? Doesn't everything fit? A murder that was to have looked like an accident – and easily would have done, if they had caught you alone, as you usually are? Read it again. From Windsor, from a courtier... Have you any notion who it could have been?"

"On my soul, Renold, I can't make a guess."

"Then the danger is all the greater. Clearly this unknown enemy won't let the matter rest. There'll be a second attempt."

Ravenwood nodded. He looked very calm. He no longer argued. "I wonder what is best to do."

"There's one easy solution."

"What?"

"Keep away from court. And let the word leak out, you are taken up entirely with your estates and the new castle. You have given up any dream of making a name at court. I fancy then you will be left undisturbed."

Ravenwood gave an amused little snort. "I said just now, 'you know me'. And you know well, I am not to be scared off like that."

"I never doubted you. Now," said Mandeville briskly, "in what way can I help you? Because you are going to need help."

"Yes. There was one service I was going to ask you, even before you arrived today."

"Ask!" Mandeville spread his hands expansively.

"Something only you can do for me. Buy me a picture."

"A picture?" The pointed jaw dropped in comical surprise. "A picture – for *you*? Since when did you care for paintings?"

"It can be quite small, but rare and exquisite. I want it to give to the King."

Six *Hampton Court*

As Ravenwood explained his purpose, Anthony's estimate of him went up. For a newcomer to court, he seemed to have sized up the situation very shrewdly.

King Charles had been taught by his father to believe that he was appointed by God to govern. In practice, being aware of his own human shortcomings, he would accept other men's advice.

"But the devil of it is," said Ravenwood, "he doesn't ask it from the *best* of his subjects, only the ones he knows and likes."

To influence him, you had somehow to enter the circle of his friends. Ability, experience, knowledge, were all quite secondary.

"I think I know something about the people of this country," his lordship went on, "and what irks them. Restriction of trade, unfair fines and taxes, the corruption that goes on in the King's name but utterly unknown to him – corruption in high places, that he *needs* to know of—"

"I am sure you do," said Mandeville with a sympathetic nod, "but all your knowledge won't win you five minutes of His Majesty's attention."

"Yet when I talked to him of horse-breeding—"

"Precisely."

Ravenwood had decided that, if he could not win the King's favour for the right reasons, he must try to do so for the wrong ones. Or at least the irrelevant.

That was why he was pressing on so urgently with his new castle. Once it was fit to receive a royal guest, his splendid stables and the race-course he was laying out might tempt the King westwards to visit him. If you wanted to break into the inner circle you must have a palatial country home in which to entertain him.

Until then, he must impress His Majesty as best he could.

"He loves gifts. He has this passion for paintings."

"And you want to give him one?"

Ravenwood looked a little shamefaced. "It sounds absurd, coming from me. And ... unworthy. But if one plays this game one has to play by the rules."

"It's the only way. Leave it to me, Will. I'll find you something that will please him. How long can you give me?"

"Three weeks? I've other business in town. I must go up when this leg is healed."

"Then I'll leave tomorrow," Mandeville promised. "The right picture won't be found in five minutes." Anthony noted the new gleam in the lively brown eye.

Ravenwood pressed them to make their headquarters at his town house near the palace. After years of neglect the family mansion was being refurbished to receive him on his more frequent visits to London. Mandeville thanked him, but said that he would rather work from his own humble lodging off Fleet Street until Ravenwood himself arrived.

"Buying a work of art can be a delicate matter. If you're known to be acting for a person of rank, the price soars."

Behind his light manner Anthony sensed the old evasive instinct. Mandeville's odd preference for two shabby rooms over a pie-shop in Hangingsword Alley carried some real advantages. In that disreputable district he had contacts, through Tobias Fludd, with a variety of characters who, though certainly not orna-

61

mental, were often extremely useful.

So next morning they took the London road. Raven-wood promised to observe all proper precautions and not to go out alone, though it seemed unlikely that a similar attempt on his life would be made again. Every man on the estate would now be alert for suspicious-looking strangers.

Anthony still found it hard to believe that anyone would go as far as murder to stop a rival in the competition for royal favour. Slander and intrigue, yes, bribery and blackmail perhaps, but — assassination? In England? In bygone days certainly, but surely not now?

Mandeville laughed at his innocence. The English nobility could be as ruthless as anyone if they were driven by greed — and even more if driven by fear. Usually, though, they got their way without violence.

On the long ride to London Mandeville talked vehem-ently about the aspects of palace life that disgusted him. Charles had cleansed his court of many abuses that had degraded it in James's day. On the surface everything was well ordered, proper and elegant, in keeping with the King's honour. Under that veneer, unknown to him, much of the old evil survived.

Few went to court with Ravenwood's unselfish motives. The place was like a gambling-house, where adventurers played at high stakes for the royal favours that would repay them with interest. It was not the court appointments that brought profit in themselves — you were lucky if you ever drew the salary that went with the post, and you were far more likely to be out of pocket. But His Majesty, himself always short of money, made it up to you in other ways.

In return for a lump sum he might assign to you the right to collect the taxes over a wide area of his kingdom. With luck, you would extract twice what you had paid him, and keep the difference yourself. Or, though Parliament had long ago made monopolies illegal, he would confer on you a "patent" that was just as good. "Like the sole right," said Mandeville, "to manufacture copper pins. Or beaver hats. You need never *make* a pin, or a hat. But everyone who does so for a living must then pay you for a licence to do so!" That was how former favourites like the Duke of Buckingham had risen from nothing to immense wealth and power. And there were all kinds of other perquisites an enterprising courtier might pick up, things that His Majesty was unaware of and never intended.

"So you see, a blunt fellow like my Lord Ravenwood is about as welcome as a cat among pigeons. He's not after profit for himself – he's rich already. For the same reason, he can't be bribed. As there's no scandal in his private life that would shock the King, he can't be blackmailed. So, if you're desperate enough, what can you do? Left alone, he'll ruin the game for everyone. You wish he'd go away, but he doesn't. You wish he'd fall ill or meet with an accident. He doesn't. So you begin to wonder, can't you somehow help things along? Once you begin to wonder, ideas present themselves."

"I can't believe they're all like that, sir!"

"They aren't. But it needs only one, doesn't it? It's that one we have to look out for."

Anthony had no answer. Someone had written that letter to Ruthin, someone alarmed by Ravenwood's developing friendship with the King. But who? In that ambitious, unscrupulous company there must be more than one with strong reasons to fear his lordship's outspoken honesty.

Once back in London, Anthony saw less of his master. There was not much for him to do. Tobias, for all his uncouthness, was an efficient valet. As the Basseys lived in Knightrider Street, only quarter of an hour's walk from Hangingsword Alley, Anthony had leave as usual to sleep at home. He had merely to report for duty each morning and be available for any service

63

required.

For the next few weeks, however, Mandeville mostly went his own way unattended, seldom divulging his plans. Anthony could only guess, from his choice of clothes, whether he was dining with someone of quality or flitting unobtrusively through the lowest haunts of the city's underworld. Though usually in his master's confidence, he had learned not to take offence when, for some reason, he was kept in the dark.

Early in his employment he had been taught a favourite motto of Tobias: a secret was like a purse of gold, best shared with as few as possible.

It was likely that the quest for the picture might involve dealing with some slippery individuals, men shy of disclosing their identity, who wanted no unnecessary witnesses.

Just two weeks had elapsed when, one morning, as he reached the rickety outside staircase climbing to Mandeville's rooms from the pie-shop yard, he met Tobias carrying down their baggage. His lordship had arrived last night at Ravenwood House. They were moving at once. Tobias had a hackney coach waiting at the end of the alley.

Anthony ran up the stairs. Mandeville handed him a flattish oblong item, hard-edged but light to hold, carefully stitched up in canvas. There was no need to ask what it was.

He nursed it gingerly as the coach nosed its jerky way along the crowded Strand.

Ravenwood House was one of the smaller of the noblemen's mansions lining the south side of that thoroughfare. It did not compare with the flamboyant splendour of Somerset House, copied from a French château, or with more recent buildings like Northampton House, its pepperpot turrets and the proud lion high above its gatehouse silhouetted against the scudding clouds.

His lordship welcomed them in his panelled study, where a fine bow window framed the southward bend of the river.

"Ah, you have it!"

He seized a penknife, cut the coarse threads and drew the picture from its covering. Peeping from behind, Anthony saw a delicate Flemish landscape in a gilded frame. Though his father always declared that the greatest painters were Italians – and most of them Venetians at that – Anthony knew that he was looking at a little masterpiece. This sort of picture the Flemings did supremely well.

"You think His Majesty will like it?" asked Ravenwood breathlessly.

"I am sure he will," said Mandeville. "This artist died young – there are not many of his paintings. I doubt if the King himself could have found one easily."

"And where did *you*?"

"In a seamen's tavern near Tower Wharf. I fancy it came through Antwerp. It's often a mistake to ask too many questions. Just 'how much?' After a few drinks I got it cheap."

"I'm truly grateful. I'll have it stitched up again, with a wrapper of fine velvet. We'll take it tomorrow."

"You know the King has left Whitehall? He's at Hampton Court."

Ravenwood nodded. "I know. It will be a pleasant drive."

They set off in good time the next morning, Anthony sitting with his back to the horses and the precious package on his lap. Facing him, the two young gentlemen exchanged their news. The work at Crucorney was going forward famously. The architect would make sure that the men did not slacken their efforts while his lordship was away. Mandeville, for his part, retailed the latest talk of town, while his friend snorted indignantly or laughed at his acid comments. Anthony could tell, however, that Ravenwood was deeply concerned about the misgovernment of the country.

The fine spring weather had hardened the roads and they made good time, reaching the palace well before noon. "We'll go back by boat," Ravenwood decided. With the stream helping the oarsmen it would be delightful to glide down the winding Thames in the evening. So, when they were set down in the outer court, facing the impressive frontage of weathered brick, its roofline clustered with towers and turrets, cupolas and glittering weathervanes, the coach was sent back to London and one footman remained to arrange for a comfortable boat to be ready at the landing-place at six o'clock.

Then, still limping slightly from his wound, Ravenwood led the way across the moat. Mandeville stalked beside him, negligent hand on sword-hilt, very debonair. Anthony kept a few respectful paces behind them, clutching the velvet-shrouded picture. With luck it would be his passport to the King's presence. Peers of the realm did not carry their own gifts. He squared his shoulders, mustering all his dignity.

Over the bridge then, venturing only sidelong glances at the King's Beasts carved in stone, lion and leopard, greyhound and griffin, dragon and hart and unicorn... Under the arch of the high-soaring gatehouse, across the base court to a second gatehouse, into the smaller quadrangle beyond. So many people, passing in and out...

Ravenwood wavered a moment, at a loss. Mandeville whispered. Now they struck confidently across the inner court to its far corner. A staircase, magnificently wide, led up to a vast echoing guard room. There were splendidly uniformed Yeomen with halberds, their little axe-blades bright as mirrors.

Now the first presence chamber... Painted ceilings of brilliant blue, fretted with complex patterns in gold... More gold, and silver, glittering from the walls... Tapestries, canopies, silken hangings... As Mandeville had promised, Hampton Court must truly be the most glorious of all the royal palaces.

No less decorative were the fine gentlemen here, with their curled hair and beards, their lovelocks so artlessly trained, their clothes a ripple of colours, velvets and satins of rose and light blue, cream and softest olive green. And all the lace, at collar and cuff and boot-top, and the ribboned canes, and the sweeping ostrich plumes...

Anthony had wondered sometimes at Mandeville's disdain of courtiers. Now, as they edged their way slowly through the throng, he understood. Such a twittering of affected, emphatic voices ... such aggressive, self-confident struttings ... such rivalry in their fine feathers... "Proud as peacocks," he would tell his father, "and noisy as parakeets!"

No one spoke to him, no one indeed looked at him, save for a few curious glances at the velvet oblong he carried. He was merely a young gentleman in attendance. For these grand folk he did not exist. He might as well have been invisible.

He moved after Ravenwood and Mandeville as they passed through into the second presence chamber. They paused, and began talking to a tall man in silver grey with a broad sash of crimson silk. Anthony caught a strong Scottish ring in his voice.

"Ah! my dear Ravenwood! A most pleasant surprise! What brings you to court again?"

Ravenwood's answer was lost in the surrounding babble. But he was presumably presenting Mandeville, for Anthony saw his master bow slightly, and, hearing the word "Marquis", he realised that here was a very grand personage indeed.

The Scotsman spoke again. "By all means! I will see what can be done. By ill chance, you have chosen a day when His Majesty is quite overwhelmed with business. However, let us see – he would be sorry to miss you—" He turned his head. Anthony saw a craggy profile, with long fair hair, silken fine and thinning already, though the Marquis was of no great age. "Sir Francis!" he called, and a lively, sly-faced gentleman hurried over to join the group. They conferred in lowered voices. Then the newcomer faced Ravenwood with an apologetic smile.

"I fear that my lord Marquis is correct. There is not a free moment for an audience."

"You see, Ravenwood?" The Scot too had an expression of cordial regret. Yet those cold, sea-blue eyes, deep set in their bony caverns, seemed to Anthony to express little cordiality. "I had hoped," the Marquis went on, "but I think we must bow to the verdict of Sir Francis Windebank." His teeth flashed. "If the Secretary of State does not know His Majesty's programme for the day, who does?"

Ravenwood held his ground. He raised his voice a little, and his words came clearly to Anthony.

"I fancy His Majesty would spare me five minutes. I have brought a small gift for him."

"Indeed?" There was a gap suddenly where Mandeville had been standing, and Anthony found himself – or rather the picture he was holding – under the frank stare of those pale eyes. "Well, you can safely leave your gift with Sir Francis."

"By all means, my Lord Ravenwood! I will place it in His Majesty's hands at the first opportunity. I am sure he will write to thank you."

"I should prefer," said Ravenwood stubbornly, "to deliver it in person."

Anthony stood, wooden-faced as he had schooled himself to look in such grand company, but the heart-beat quickened under his doublet as he wondered what way would be found round the impasse.

The three men faced each other, outwardly suave and civil. He could not see his lordship's expression, but he could imagine that his cheeks were taking on an even ruddier hue than usual.

Then, as suddenly as he had vanished, Mandeville was there again. A pleasant-looking gentleman was at his side. Anthony, who had not expected to see a familiar face here, remembered him immediately. He was Endymion Porter, the King's personal friend and trusted adviser on artistic matters. In his first days with Mandeville Anthony had delivered confidential letters to him at his home in the Strand.

Mandeville presented him to Ravenwood. "My lord!" cried Mr Porter exuberantly. "Sir Renold tells me you have a picture for His Majesty!"

"I understand that he is too occupied to receive me."

Mr Porter's eyes flickered briefly round their faces. "He *is* somewhat busy today," he said diplomatically, "but he can always make time to look at a painting." Anthony thought he heard a little snort of impatience from the Marquis. "Indeed," Mr Porter continued, with a disarming smile in the Scot's direction, "it would be a brave man who kept you from his presence. You will recall, Sir Renold was of particular service to the King over the matter of the Castelrosso collection. His Majesty has given orders, in any matter connected with the arts, that Sir Renold is always to be granted access."

There was nothing more to be said. The Marquis shrugged his shoulders and turned away. The Secretary of State looked daggers at Mandeville and dropped back. Blandly Mr Porter conducted his lordship's little party through the audience chamber into the King's withdrawing room beyond.

Anthony had several times seen His Majesty from a distance on public occasions. Only now, at close quarters, did he realise how small Charles Stuart was, and yet with what extraordinary dignity he bore himself among these taller men.

There were not many in this inner apartment. The King was chatting with two, Nicholas Lanier, as Anthony learnt afterwards, the Master of the King's Music, and Sir Henry Herbert, the Master of the Revels, a play-script in his hand. These two moved aside at the approach of the new arrivals. It was interesting to note how the King's rather mournful face lit up with interest as he recognised them.

"Ravenwood! An unexpected pleasure! And Mande-ville!"

Another Scottish voice... Though he had left his native country at the age of three, Charles had never lost the pronunciation learnt in early childhood. But of course his father's court, and now his own, had always been full of fellow-countrymen.

He spoke too with a slight impediment. Hardly a stammer, but a hesitation, which made him a man of few words, very different from the glib courtiers surrounding him.

Anthony was beckoned forward to display the paint-ing.

"This is young Mr Bassey," said Mandeville swiftly. "He was of great help to me – indeed, he showed great courage and faced many dangers – when Your Majesty honoured me with the mission to Castelrosso."

"I am obliged to you, Mr – er – Mr—" the King said mechanically, but his mind, like his eyes, was intent upon the object Anthony held.

It was slightly awkward, clutching his hat and striving to uncover the picture with a fitting flourish. He succeeded however, and the slow raising of the royal eyebrows, the still further brightening of those hooded eyes, were ample compensation for the nervous stress.

"Exquisite," said the King huskily. "Take it nearer to the window, Mr – er – Mr—"

Anthony moved over with him, careful to keep the

painting out of the dazzling sunshine that streamed through the glass.

All the gentlemen clustered round with admiring comments. Mr Porter led the chorus. Ravenwood beamed and strove to hide his embarrassment as he was complimented upon his taste.

No doubt whatever, this part of his calculated strategy to win the King's goodwill had been a triumphant success.

Anthony's role was played. There was no further place for him in this exalted gathering. His valuable burden was taken from him, and Ravenwood nodded his dismissal. He remembered to retire from the room backwards, bowing three times at proper intervals in the direction of his sovereign. The King seemed quite oblivious of his departure, but Mandeville murmured from the corner of his mouth: "Well done! Six o'clock then, on the barge walk."

Anthony was left with a long April afternoon to pass alone.

He had not traversed Europe without learning to look after himself, nor known the resourceful Tobias without picking up further tips on the craft of comfortable survival. Hampton Court, though not such a labyrinth as Whitehall, was a big enough place for no one to know everybody. Once clear of the presence chambers where the nobility congregated, he had only to walk with a confident, unhesitating step as though he knew where he was going and was under orders from some magnificent unknown. Following his nose, quite literally, he came to a hall where dinner was being served at long tables. A quick glance round, assessing the dress and deportment of the company, confirmed that this was where petty officials, superior servants and others of his own humble rank could stay the pangs of hunger while awaiting the pleasure of their betters. He was himself, after all, in attendance upon my Lord Ravenwood. So, with a conscience as good as his appetite, he slipped into a vacant seat and was quickly served.

The meal over, it was good to escape from the hall, reeking of hot food and humanity. The palace had acres of gardens where he could wander at will. He looked up at the famous clock, which showed not only hour, day and month, but even the time of high tide at London Bridge. He had still five clear hours.

On such a fair afternoon the gardens were almost as crowded as the galleries. Ladies and gentlemen were strolling about the vast formal chequerboard of small lawns and ponds and squares of white sand. Others were exploring the alleys where the branches, trained as arches overhead, were putting forth their spring foliage to dapple the paths with shade. Bred in the narrow streets around St Paul's, Anthony could not put a name to everything, but he knew the wallflowers and cows-lips, the tulips and peonies, and the fragrant white double violets. The lilac was coming out, and there were clouds of blossom, cherry and plum and damascene.

A little self-conscious, being alone, he drifted by instinct towards the more distant, unfrequented parts, until there was not another person in sight. He walked on, more at ease, feeling freer to look about him. But this agreeable solitude was not his to enjoy for long.

From behind a tall hedge of clipped yew he heard the strains of a violin. He stopped in his tracks, memories flooding into his head. The music, this stately measure, a Spanish dance – what was it called? A saraband?

He would never forget where he had first heard that tune, played as now by a single fiddler. Every note brought back that dry, herb-scented Italian summer in the mysterious cliff garden overhanging the battlements of Castelrosso.

There was an archway in the hedge, with two steps up to a light wicket-gate, invitingly ajar. He ran forward impulsively, and plunged through. The music came

72

from the left, and turning his head he looked down a long paved vista.

A lady was sitting on a marble seat. Several others were circling before her, dancing the saraband. But it was to the violinist that his eyes flew.

He was a tiny figure. Not a true dwarf, but a perfectly proportioned midget, perhaps four feet tall. Dark, sallow, Italian – and a most skilled musician. It could only be—

"Zorzi!" cried Anthony.

Luckily the music and the laughter, and the vast distances of the palace garden, did much to mute the noise of his interruption. The violinist went on playing, unchecked. The ladies continued to revolve in the measures of the dance. But one, whose place in the ring happened to bring her nearest to him as he called, twirled, came face to face with him, and faltered as their eyes met.

She gasped. Her lips framed: "*Anthony!*" but any sound was lost. Then, with a grimace of warning, she spun round with a graceful flourish of petticoats, and continued with the evolutions of the saraband.

A heavy hand fell on Anthony's shoulder. A shocked voice hissed in his ear: "Sir! This is the Queen's Privy Garden!" A mountainous Yeoman of the Guard hauled him back through the archway. In those few confused moments he had a final impression of the ladies still dancing round. The one on the marble bench had not even looked up. Firmly ejected, with the wicket-gate slammed behind him and the outraged guard glaring balefully over it, Anthony stumbled away down the steps, going hot and cold by turns.

The seated lady must have been Queen Henrietta Maria herself. And, just as surely, the dark girl had been Amoret Grisedale. No doubt of that, although – odd to think of it – he had never seen her in skirts before.

Of course. Mandeville had told him. Her distracted

grandmother, no longer able to cope with her, had managed to pack her off to court. She was a Maid of Honour.

A wave of sadness washed over him. Always beyond his reach, Amoret was now even more hopelessly removed from his own station of life. He had never seriously expected to see her again. Now he must not even try to.

He wandered away disconsolately, not sorry to lose himself again among the strollers in the more frequented parts of the gardens. He now wanted only to get away from Hampton Court and its glories. But the afternoon still stretched before him, dull and seemingly endless as the broad walk along which he was striding, scowling and only with difficulty restraining himself from kicking the gravel as he went.

Then suddenly, from somewhere far behind him, that damned fiddle again! A brief flourish of high notes, ending abruptly as a trumpet-call.

In spite of himself, he looked back. There was no more music. It had sounded like an urgent signal. It *was* a signal. From a balustraded terrace far behind him a diminutive figure was frantically waving.

Zorzi! There could be no harm in speaking with Zorzi. After all they had once gone through together in Italy it would be unforgivably ungrateful.

He hurried back and Zorzi came skipping down from the terrace to meet him. Under the amused gaze of the passers-by, they clasped hands affectionately.

"Your pardon, Mr Bassey, for the discourtesy!" Zorzi's English had made great progress since his arrival in England.

"Discourtesy?" echoed Anthony.

"That I play the music after you! But it would have been worse to shout. And with my short legs I should never have caught up with you." He glanced round at the people walking past them, and dropped into Italian.

"I have a message from a certain lady. I was to find you—" he paused and chuckled—"if it meant tearing the palace apart. *I*!"

Seven *Maid of Honour*

The Honourable Amoret Grisedale had been as startled as Anthony by that unexpected confrontation.

She knew him instantly. Though he had grown taller and filled out, and there was a delicate dark shadow pencilled on his upper lip, he was unmistakably Anthony Bassey.

In the moment that she knew him she realised that she must not know him. Not here, of all places. Explanations would be demanded, and her secret would be out. It would be impossible to hide the fact that they had met in Italy. Yet, as all the world was given to understand, she had never set foot outside England.

Hence the appealing look she flashed at him. Whether or not he was as quick-witted as he had shown himself in the old days, he was given no chance to blurt out a syllable that would have betrayed her. Never before had she been so thankful for the vigilance of the guard. She saw poor Anthony pounced upon and hustled through the gate. With her deep relief was mingled a pang of regret.

Anthony – here! Perhaps Mandeville was not far away?

"Come, ladies, it is time for more serious matters."

The Queen's voice, rather charming with its strong French intonation, brought the impromptu dance to an immediate stop. She rose, handing her embroidery-frame to the nearest lady-in-waiting, and turned towards the palace. They all fell in behind her, docile as sheep.

In an hour Her Majesty was to see her confessor. It was fortunate, thought Amoret, that Her Majesty, while frivolous in many ways, was devout in her Roman Catholic faith. Once she had been escorted back to her apartments she would have no further need of Amoret's services for the remainder of the afternoon.

There was just time for a hurriedly whispered instruction to Zorzi. It was all right to be seen talking to Zorzi. At the Queen's wish she was supposed to be helping him with his English. The other Maids of Honour had little or no Italian.

Zorzi must find Anthony at once. "Bring him to Mirefleur! I will get there as soon as I can."

Zorzi bowed and slipped away. Amoret hastened after the other ladies. A Maid of Honour must not be seen to run. Decorum, dignity, were the watchwords at court. She made a face. No one was near enough to see that.

Mirefleur... She smiled now at her choice of a meeting-place. In the heat of the moment it was the first idea that had flashed into her mind. There was a certain humour about it.

The old garden tower was one of several built by King Henry when, a hundred years ago, he had taken the palace from his fallen minister, Cardinal Wolsey. They had been sited in secluded places, convenient accommodation for any young woman with whom Henry was carrying on a secret love-affair. He himself, it was said, had composed the verse scratched on a window with a diamond ring:

> *Within this tower*
> *There lieth a flower*
> *That hath my heart.*

Amoret herself, in her earliest days at court, had been

bidden to a rendezvous at Mirefleur. She had the letter still. It was, she supposed, the first love-letter she had ever received – if it deserved that name. Anyhow, she had kept it as a curiosity. She had not answered it, much less kept the assignation.

Before going to court she had been warned by her grandmother – as though she were a child who needed such warning! – that she must be on her guard against the men she would meet there. On her arrival, the Queen had said the same. "While you are here," the little Frenchwoman had impressed upon her, "you are under my care – as if I were your mother, as well as your queen. One hint of scandal, pouf! You would have to go. My ladies must be above suspicion. So, my child, whatever the temptation . . ."

"Yes, madam," Amoret had said. She could be meek enough when meekness was called for.

The Marquis of Lockerbie was a temptation easy to resist. She did not dislike Scotsmen. They had a certain novelty about them that appealed to her natural curiosity. She was not prejudiced against older men. Indeed, she often found them more interesting to talk to than young sprigs as empty-headed as her brother. But instinctively she distrusted Lockerbie and was repelled by him.

The older ladies-in-waiting, though knowing nothing of that letter, had not failed to observe his usual discreet preliminaries, and Lady Dalkeith, herself a Scot, had advised Amoret to be careful.

"That man is a complete hypocrite. He makes a show of his religion. With the King he is a great admirer of the Church of England and pretends he would like to see all the same rituals in our Kirk at home. Yet when he talks with the Queen he leads her on to hope that she may convert him to her own Roman church." Lady Dalkeith sniffed. "In actual fact Lockerbie cares for neither God nor man – but a deal too much for woman! He is a goat, though their Majesties cannot see the cloven feet. Keep away from him, my dear. Every pretty young woman who appears at court—" She paused eloquently.

Even without that advice Amoret would not have been such a fool as to visit the garden tower in the gloaming of a November afternoon. At her next meeting with Lockerbie his chilly eyes had glared angrily from their deep sockets. He was a proud man, he had been snubbed, and he made no further advances. She realised that she had acquired an enemy. How dangerous an enemy became apparent as the months passed and she learned more about him. Lockerbie had a ruthless reputation. He would stick at nothing.

Luckily for her, he had higher ambitions than the mere seduction of a young girl. He was intent upon strengthening his position with the King. "He is one of those who favour the iron hand in government, like Tom Wentworth," explained Lady Dalkeith. "And with Wentworth made Lord Deputy in Ireland, he schemes to slip into his place with the King. Woe betide anyone who gets in his way! And woe betide England – and Scotland too – if the King listens to him. He would have His Majesty act like a dictator to his subjects."

Lockerbie had no further place in Amoret's thoughts when, the Queen safely settled with a book of devotions to await her confessor, she was able to slip back into the gardens and make her way to the sequestered corner where Mirefleur stood.

Had Zorzi managed to track Anthony down in the rambling vastness of the grounds? Her heart leapt with delight as she crossed the threshold and saw them sitting on the stone window-seat, chattering like magpies in a mixture of English and Italian.

They jumped to their feet as her shadow fell between them. Anthony swept off his hat and started towards her, then stopped hesitantly. Amoret felt no such hesitation. She flung her arms round him and kissed him full on the mouth.

"Anthony! This is most wonderful!"

"My lady—" he stammered.

"My lady be damned," she said, releasing him. "You did not call me that in Italy."

He laughed. "When anyone was listening, I had to call you 'my lord'."

"And when anyone is listening you must call me 'my lady' now, I suppose. But if you stand on such ceremony in private I shall call *you* 'Mr Bassey'." She turned to the dwarf who was moving to the doorway. "Thank you for finding him, Zorzi. There is no need to go."

"It is better I watch outside. The signore and I have already talked together. Now it is your turn." He smiled and stepped out into the sunshine.

She sat down and Anthony took his place beside her. "You're a great lady now," he said shyly.

She ignored that. "*You*'ve become quite the fine young gentleman."

"How are things with you – Amoret? Are you happy in this life?"

She wrinkled up her nose in mock disgust. "Sometimes. And sometimes I could scream. The tedium. The stiffness. The formality."

She had meant to talk about other things. But his question, and his obvious sympathy, undammed the frustration of the past six months. For the next few minutes it all poured out.

The court atmosphere stifled her. She was bored by the long ceremonies, the endless hours of sitting with hateful needlework or playing brainless card games, and the tittle-tattle that passed for conversation.

She was infuriated, above all, by the general assumption that, because of her sex, she had neither knowledge nor intellect. The King might be surrounded by interesting men – some of them, at any rate – poets, music-lovers, connoisseurs of the arts, dabblers in the sciences.

But such people seldom came within her reach. If they did, she got little encouragement to take an active part in their discussions. She was expected to cast her eyes down, look demure, and be patronised with a casual compliment.

"Like a bone thrown to a dog!" she said stormily.

"Do you enjoy none of it?"

"I enjoy the dancing. And the plays – I wish the actors came more often." Her eyes shone. "The Christmas revels were wonderful." She added proudly, "I had a part in the masque. A nymph. Even the King joins in the masque at Christmas. And the Queen, of course. Luckily for us, she adores masques."

Anthony did not ask what costume she had worn. She did not really mind his slowness, because she was impatient to ask about Mandeville.

"That is enough about me," she said. "What are *you* doing here?"

"I came from London this morning with Lord Raven-wood."

Her face fell. She could not help it. "Have you left Sir Renold?" she asked incredulously.

"Oh, *no*! He's here too. I left them with the King. I have to meet them at six o'clock. We're going back by water."

"Oh." Her voice was suddenly flat. "Will you be here again?"

He laughed. "Does one ever know – with Mande-ville?"

She questioned him about their doings during the past year. She knew she would not be told the half of it. If Anthony prattled of his master's more private business, even to her, he would not stay long in Mandeville's employment. Even so, compared with her own colour-less existence, Anthony's life sounded enviably full of incident.

She was particularly interested to learn that they had

just been up to Herefordshire. Mandeville's mother must be formidable, but in a way fascinating. It would be stimulating, if also unnerving, to cross swords with her.

"And this Lord Ravenwood you came with?"

An old friend of Mandeville's, Anthony explained, who was presenting a picture to the King.

She had a feeling that there was rather more to it than that. She probed delicately but with determination. Anthony admitted that Lord Ravenwood was anxious to win His Majesty's favour.

"Men who bring him gifts usually are!"

Anthony wavered, shrugged, and supposed there was no secret about it. Ravenwood was more anxious than most, and he had the most honourable reasons. Anthony proceeded to enlarge upon them.

She nodded approvingly. "He is right. There's a need for men like him at court."

She was not sure that Anthony had told her everything. No matter. Somehow she would find out. For the moment, though, she was absorbed by the immediate problem, drawn into it herself as though into some intriguing game of skill.

"There is another way to please the King," she suggested.

"How?"

"To please the Queen. He is devoted to her." She considered. "Your Lord Ravenwood wants to show off his new castle. But it's difficult – Herefordshire is rather far. They make a royal progress every summer, staying at great houses. But the programmes tend to follow a strict pattern, year by year – a pattern laid down by precedent. Oh, that word, 'precedent'!" She rolled her eyes comically. "To extend the itinerary as far west as Crucorney – I think only one thing would persuade His Majesty. If it were to please the Queen."

"And what *would* please her? What are her tastes?"

Amoret was suddenly inspired. "I told you – she adores masques. Much more than plays. Her English is not good enough to follow plays. But masques! Music, dancing, wonderful costumes, magical stage effects—" She looked at Anthony and knew that he was beginning to catch her enthusiasm. "If Lord Ravenwood could have his new castle ready by August – if he prepared some truly gorgeous entertainment to mark the occasion – I think she would find it irresistible."

The idea was racing away with her. But before she could develop it in detail, Zorzi called from the doorway:

"Someone is coming, my lady!"

Amoret choked back an unladylike exclamation. There was a tension in Zorzi's voice suggesting that instant action was advisable.

"You'd better go, Anthony. We mustn't be seen together."

There would be the devil to pay if they were. A Maid of Honour was expected to behave like a nun.

"To the left, signore," said Zorzi, his watchful eyes turned to the right.

Anthony looked back from the doorway, made a helpless gesture of regret, turned to the left, and was gone.

She sat down again, an emptiness in her heart she had never imagined she could feel. Zorzi came in and sat where Anthony had been. "I think – my lesson in English, perhaps?" he prompted her.

"Of course."

She composed her features just in time. The door darkened. A Scottish voice spoke. "Ah! The *most* Honourable Amoret – with her musical manikin." She looked up to see the unwelcome face bowed mockingly over her.

"Yes, my Lord Marquis. I am giving Signor Zorzi another English lesson – as Her Majesty commanded.

English as spoken in *polite* society. Would you care to join us?"

He ignored her sarcasm. "So – you found your way to Mirefleur? At last."

"Yes, my lord. I thought it would be a good place for our study – you once recommended it as a spot where one need fear no tiresome interruptions. It seems that your lordship was mistaken."

It was said that Lockerbie did not know how to blush. That too was a mistake. But of course a flush of fury was hardly a blush of shame.

"You must have been interrupted a great deal this afternoon," he said roughly.

"Oh, no."

"I saw a young man just now, walking away very rapidly—"

"Indeed?" She was all innocence. "Who was he?"

"I have no idea. I have seen him somewhere before. I caught only a glimpse of his back – but I could have sworn he came out of this doorway."

"Surely not! Signor Zorzi, have *you* seen a young man here?"

"Here? No, my lady."

She smiled sweetly at the Marquis. "Then for the second time your lordship was mistaken. And now, if you will excuse us, we had better continue with our lesson."

Eight *The Masque of Pegasus*

Even with muscular boatmen, a fast-running stream, and in the later stages a helpful ebb-tide, it seemed a long way back. Cool, as the sunshine lifted from the river and the western sky took fire. Chillier, as darkness came down, and lighted windows blossomed pale yellow in the bankside villages. There were stretches where the blackness was broken only by the torches and lanterns of other craft and their own, and by the tiny red dragon's eye of Ravenwood's glowing pipe, where he sat snug under the canopy with Mandeville, talking in a low voice of their day.

The two gentlemen seemed well satisfied. The King had been gracious. Whatever the supposed pressures of business, he had detained them in leisurely conversation. He had expressed regret that Ravenwood lived so far away and came to court so seldom. This had given Ravenwood the cue to sing the praises of Herefordshire and make discreet mention of his ambitious projects at Crucorney. Despite these, he was quick to add, he planned to come out into the world more often – and was, needless to say, always at His Majesty's service.

After that, Anthony gathered, they had spent the afternoon making themselves agreeable to old acquaintances and new, my Lord This and Sir Somebody That, who might be useful – or obstructive – in the months ahead.

Though in no sense shut out of the conversation,

Anthony had to pick up its drift by catching at clues and oblique references. In a hired boat from Hampton Court one must guard against saying anything that might be repeated elsewhere. For all their lowered voices, the creak of rowlocks, the steady splash and suck of oars, Ravenwood and Mandeville wrapped up their talk so that nothing too private would reach the ears of the rowers.

It was almost midnight when at last, over a more than welcome supper of cold venison pasty and Westphalia ham, they could talk freely.

"Lockerbie is our man," declared Mandeville. This was the name, Anthony now realised, of the Scottish marquis they had met in the presence chamber.

"There were others even less pleased to see me," said Ravenwood doubtfully.

"They were clumsier at concealing it. No, for all his civility, he was determined to keep you away from the King. Windebank merely took his cue from Lockerbie. 'Whirly Windebank', as the ballad calls him," said Mandeville with amused contempt. "He is turning all the time, just as the wind blows."

Other courtiers might have been equally unhelpful – they were instinctively jealous of any newcomer – but only the Marquis filled the bill in all respects. Of all the King's inner circle he was, at the present time, the most ambitious and the least secure. Unlike the others, content to hold their positions, he was playing for much higher stakes. He aimed not at mere money or at honours. He wanted power. And his ruthless character equipped him for the fight to win it.

That afternoon, while Ravenwood had been chatting with his fellow peers, Mandeville had made some more intimate inquiries from people he could trust. Their answers had confirmed his theory.

"He thinks himself the rising star – since Tom Wentworth was sent off to Dublin. That removed his great obstacle. With Black Tom still at the King's elbow, Lockerbie would not have got this far. Black Tom would see to that! He's another man of steel – but you can respect him even when you disagree. He has something that Lockerbie hasn't got. Integrity. But he's far away, trying to keep the peace in Ireland, and God knows when he'll be back. Meanwhile, Lockerbie makes hay while the sun shines. You, my dear Will, look to him like a black rain-cloud coming up from the West." He poured himself another glass of wine, noticed Anthony stifling a yawn, and told him he could go to bed.

Anthony rose thankfully and made his formal bow to his lordship. Considerately, if somewhat late in the day, Ravenwood inquired how Anthony had passed the afternoon.

"I walked in the gardens, my lord." Anthony paused at the door and added casually, to his master. "I met Amoret Grisedale."

"The devil you did!" Only for a few seconds was Mandeville shaken out of his usual self-command. Recovering, he went on in a casual tone to match Anthony's, "You must tell me about it tomorrow."

Anthony bowed again, and withdrew. He might have known how hard it was to win with Mandeville.

The next morning, however, giving the gentlemen a full description of his encounter, he found an attentive audience. Ravenwood was especially intrigued.

"Who *is* this young lady?"

"The granddaughter of the seventh Lord Grisedale," Mandeville explained. "Her young brother is the eighth baron – their father died young. A Derbyshire family originally. They still have land there, I believe, but the main estates are in Kent. Being orphans, they've been brought up there by the grandmother."

With this smooth flow of factual detail he washed over, Anthony noted with amusement, any other matters better not disclosed. Old friend Ravenwood might be, but he was not going to be told about Amoret's share in the Castelrosso adventure.

His lordship, fortunately, was far more interested in the future. He grew excited. In this girl, odd and unconventional though she sounded, he might find another useful friend at court – and in a quarter where as yet he had no allies, among the Queen's ladies.

"This notion of hers – a masque! Is there anything in it, Renold?"

"There'd be a great deal. But you can't possibly have your castle finished by the end of this summer."

"Not *finished*. The embellishments will take years. But fit to show off to their Majesties. If we press on," said Ravenwood vigorously. "If need be, I will pay the men extra to work by lantern-light. The Little Castle can be furnished, the Banqueting Hall and the Great Gallery can be ready, most of the courtiers can be accommodated in the Priory—"

"You are a demon for energy," said Mandeville with a laugh. "I can see why you need the whole nation's business to absorb it."

"I can promise Crucorney. But how do I put on a masque?" His lordship's confidence failed like a snuffed-out candle. "I know nothing about such things."

"There's no problem. If you have the money."

"The money is nothing."

Again Mandeville laughed. "Wait till you get the bills."

Ravenwood, he explained, had simply to commission a poet and a designer. These men would devise the entertainment from start to finish. Though the estate would provide timber and other materials, and much of the ordinary labour needed, the designer would order whatever else was required, and would make subcontracts with special craftsmen – scene-painters and gilders and woodcarvers, and a host of others. The poet would engage actors to speak his lines. Though there must be scope for some of the lords and ladies to put on superb costumes and display themselves, such illustrious personages could not be expected to learn long, if any, speeches or attend tedious rehearsals. The poet would help to find a composer, if new music was wanted, and he in turn would have suggestions about singers and musicians.

"Well, how do I find a poet? And the – this other fellow?" It was all Anthony could do not to laugh at Ravenwood's worried expression.

Finding authors and designers, said Mandeville soothingly, was not difficult. There were not many, but their names were well known.

Ravenwood knew of two. Ben Jonson and Inigo Jones. They were the best, weren't they? He wanted the best.

"Yes. But they quarrelled years ago and haven't worked together since. Poor Ben is a sick man, and may write no more. Jones is very busy. Remember, he's also Surveyor to His Majesty's Works. He'll produce the royal masques, of course. It's rare now for him to take a commission from anyone else."

"We must get him." Ravenwood's determination flooded back. "Perhaps this young lady – this Amoret of yours – can use her wiles upon him."

Even as he spoke, however, the said young lady was enduring an uncomfortable half-hour alone with the Queen, and her prospects of exercising any future influence at court appeared dim.

"So – you deny this story?"

"Absolutely, madam."

Henrietta Maria sat up straight, dignified yet ill at ease. Amoret, debarred from taking a stool on such a formal occasion, stood before her like a prisoner on trial.

The Queen's expression of moral disapproval went incongruously with those liquid eyes, the fringe of little ringlet curls she herself had made so fashionable, and her reputation for unconventional frivolity.

For a wild moment Amoret was tempted to tell the exact truth of her surprise encounter with this humbly born but most respectable youth, and of the meeting, indiscreet perhaps but completely innocent, which had followed it. Surely this woman would understand? Was she not still, inside, the same high-spirited French princess who, at Amoret's age, had behaved with even less decorum? Who, as a young bride, unable any longer to bear the restrictions of palace protocol, had stolen out one evening, alone and disguised, to stare at the London shops? Who, on another occasion, locked in her room by the King, had clenched her little fist in fury and smashed a window with it?

A moment's reflection warned Amoret not to remind Her Majesty of those wilful shows of independence. And, however harmless her friendship with Anthony Bassey, it would be fatal to admit to that conversation in the tower.

"You are not carrying on any kind of affair with a young man?" the Queen persisted.

"No, madam," Amoret felt she could answer truthfully. "Who says so?" she demanded with a show of indignation.

"You must not interrogate me, child!"

"Your pardon, madam – but am I to be slandered without the chance to defend myself?"

"No, no." The Queen looked troubled. "There has perhaps been some misunderstanding."

"Indeed there has!"

"My informant is a man of honour – and of high position. It places me in some difficulty. He was quite positive. He felt I should send you away."

I'm sure he did, thought Amoret apprehensively. She had been a conceited little fool to underestimate Lockerbie. He had seized this chance to get his revenge.

"You recall, child – when you came, I warned you," continued the Queen reproachfully. "A Maid of Honour must be above scandal." She sighed. "It is impossible I call this great nobleman a liar. It is impossible I do perhaps injustice to you. Yet something I must do."

"Yes, madam?" Amoret waited with downcast eyes. For all her grumbles at court life, the last thing she wanted was to be sent home in disgrace.

Henrietta Maria's tone changed suddenly. She smiled.

"You will go away to your room, now, and prepare a request to me. You will beg leave of absence for two or three months – you yourself will think of the reason. Perhaps your grandmother is sick. Whatever the excuse, I shall graciously grant your request. So – I am not sending you away, you are going at your own request. But for a little while you will not be here, and a certain great nobleman cannot complain that I have ignored him."

"Thank you, madam. You have been very kind."

"You are very young, my dear Amoret. You must sometimes find it irksome here. The change will do you no harm. And if there is indeed some young man attracted to you – without your encouragement, of course, even without your knowledge – then your absence will give him time to turn his eyes elsewhere."

You do not believe me, thought Amoret. But because you can remember when you were my age, you are letting me down as lightly as you dare.

"You are very kind, madam," she repeated, and was glad that in curtseying she was spared meeting the Queen's eyes. She withdrew, her mind in ferment.

The odious Lockerbie had scored a point against her. Yet somehow she would retrieve the situation, turn this present discomfiture to advantage.

By the time she had reached her own room she thought she had the answer. She opened her desk, took out ink and paper, and arranged her thoughts as she sharpened her quill.

It was time that young Fabian showed his face on his Derbyshire estates. What more fitting than that his elder sister should accompany him? Especially since her own modest inheritance formed part of them – the lands that would one day be her dowry when she married. It would sound far better at court than some excuse of an ailing grandmother.

To that grandmother she began her first letter. "*Madam . . .*" Respectful, yet warmly affectionate, as always, she left no room for doubt in old Lady Grisedale's mind as to what she wanted to do, and meant to do.

The second letter took longer to compose. "*Sir . . .*" It would be wiser not to trust it to her maid – she would slip it to Zorzi for dispatch, in case a watch was kept now on her correspondence. A Maid of Honour should not be writing letters to Mad Mandeville.

This one reached Ravenwood House before dinner next day. Anthony was there when his master broke the seal, unfolded the paper, and remarked cheerfully that he would be damned. He passed it to Anthony. "You had better read this. You started it!"

Amoret had leave of absence. She was planning a journey to the North with her brother to visit the family estates there. She would like, if agreeable to Lord Ravenwood, to make a detour on the way back and see his wonderful new castle. Then, when she returned to court, she would be able to mention it to Her Majesty and rouse her interest in the proposed masque.

As I have not yet the honour of my lord's acquaintance, it would be more seemly, she continued artlessly, *if we were invited to some other neighbouring house, so that our visit to Crucorney seems by chance and not by design. Your own home at Wildhope sounds most conveniently situated. If your*—the last word had clearly begun as "*you*" and

the final letter had been tagged on as an afterthought
—*mother were to offer us hospitality for a few days – we
shall be a small party, with few servants – we should be
vastly obliged. The introduction to your neighbour could
arise most naturally.*

Anthony met his master's ironic eye. "Will you agree,
sir?"

"How can I refuse? She's a determined young
woman. We want her help, and the plan has possibil-
ities. I'll ask my mother to send her an invitation in
proper form." He laughed softly. "Lord knows what
my mother will start imagining! No matter."

Ravenwood, when told, was delighted.

"You'll have to put on that masque now," said Mandeville. "You're committed."

"Of course! And I look forward to meeting your
remarkable friend. 'A lass unparalleled'." For all his
outdoor enthusiasms Ravenwood sometimes surprised
his more bookish friends with a poetic quotation,
usually from Shakespeare.

He was now fired with the idea of this latest project.
Though he had come up to London with half a dozen
important matters of business to transact, he could not
rest until he had found an author and a designer to
undertake the masque.

Despite the proverbial poverty of writers and artists,
and his own reputation for open-handed generosity, this
proved unexpectedly difficult. Even Mandeville's wide-
reaching connections, whether at court through the
helpful Endymion Porter or with players in the public
theatre, failed to produce a poet who could write effec-
tively for the stage. Neither Will Davenant nor Aurelian
Townsend, neither Shirley nor Carew, seemed able to
accept his lordship's commission. They were honoured,
they were flattered, they regretted ... but for one
reason or another, the pressure of other work or the

remoteness of Herefordshire or the state of their health, they begged to be excused.

"Health!" growled Ravenwood. "I fancy the word has been put round, it is unhealthy to serve me in this enterprise!"

It was less surprising that, as Mandeville had prophesied, Inigo Jones was prevented by his official duties from taking on the task of designer. But at least, while declining in a rather grand manner, he was good enough to recommend a substitute, one Hugh Huntley, who had worked under him and should have skills sufficient for his lordship's needs.

With this, Ravenwood had to be satisfied. A decision must be made before he left town. In the same somewhat desperate spirit he clutched at the name of Edmund Challenor, a young gentleman who, after sharpening his wits at Oxford and Cambridge and among the lawyers at the Inns of Court, was attracting notice with his poems and plays. He had never yet written a masque, but was keen to do so.

"He's said to be ambitious," said Ravenwood, "but he's little known at court. It may be no bad thing to present their Majesties with a new name."

Both men were accordingly bidden to Ravenwood House for a preliminary discussion. As his lordship's secretary had so much other business to handle, Anthony was pressed into service to take notes of whatever was agreed.

It was Huntley who was first ushered into the study overlooking the Thames.

He almost shambled in, an unprepossessing little man, with fierce red hair where he was not balding. His small, greenish eyes were equally fierce as he surveyed the three of them, ranged behind the table with their backs to the great bow window. The fingers gripping the brim of his hat were stubby and dirt-engrained. Anthony's heart sank. It was hard to associate this rough fellow with the delicacy, the soaring fantasy, required for the designing of a masque.

"Pray be seated, Mr Huntley," said Ravenwood with his usual cordiality. The little man growled acknowledgement, pulled up a stool, and subsided upon it. "You are, I am told, a Warwickshire man?"

"Nay, Worcestershire!" The word rang almost like an indignant retort. "My lord," came as a sulky afterthought.

"Worcestershire? Better still." His lordship became more genial than ever. "Then we are neighbours. Perhaps you already know Crucorney?"

"Crucorney?" The green eyes narrowed. "This masque is to be presented at Crucorney?"

"Yes. But at the castle I am building. Not the old priory, if you were thinking—"

"It's all one to me, my lord. Castle or priory. I have never been to Crucorney. I've never set foot in Herefordshire." Mr Huntley sounded indifferent whether he ever did so or not.

When he has gone, Anthony told himself, my lord will declare that he is a blunt honest fellow, who knows his own worth and will lick no one's boots. In fact, he is uncouth, and in most houses of this quality he would soon be shown the door.

The awkward atmosphere created by these opening exchanges was lightened by the announcement of Mr Challenor. Here was a contrast indeed.

The young poet entered with the assurance of an actor. His bow was elegant, not servile but properly deferential to his lordship. A broad sash of tangerine taffeta blazed a dramatic contrast across his steel-blue suit. He crossed the room with quick, fastidious little steps. Anthony had never seen such high-heeled boots. They clicked over the floorboards like the hooves of a goat.

Mr Challenor accepted the seat offered him, laid

down his hat and ribboned cane, drew off his gloves to reveal slender, pale and exquisitely manicured hands, and produced a little roll of manuscript.

"Merely my first thoughts, my lord. The first flutterings of my Muse – best captured at once on paper."

"Your Muse loses no time," said Mandeville dryly.

"No, I was fortunate enough to receive an instant inspiration. I shall entitle my piece *The Masque of Pegasus*."

"Pegasus?" Ravenwood savoured the name approvingly.

"The winged horse of Grecian myth. A fitting theme, I think, as your lordship's interest in horses is well known. And a graceful compliment to their Majesties for the same reason."

"Excellent. What do you think of it, Renold?"

"I agree. Most promising. And the stories of Pegasus offer plenty of scope. The vision of Athene – the magic bridle she gives Bellerophon – the fatal attempt to fly to Heaven—"

"I see you are familiar with ancient literature," said Mr Challenor. He did not look exceptionally pleased.

Ravenwood thought it time to draw Huntley into the conversation. "Think you could manage that? A flying horse?"

The designer snorted. "Child's play! Gods and goddesses descending or ascending – in clouds, in chariots, or like Jupiter on the back of an eagle. It has been done countless times. The sole difficulty is to give it novelty. I like the notion of a horse," he admitted grudgingly. "And indeed, for the whole conception, the horse as theme. I like it."

"I am relieved." Mr Challenor scowled at him.

"It suggests Centaurs. I have it! An antimasque of Centaurs."

"A *what*?"

"It is usual now to have an antimasque at the beginning. You have not written a masque before, they tell me, but you can take my word for it. Since Jonson started the practice it has been the fashion. A complete contrast to all that follows. Clownishness and uncouthness," went on Huntley, as if blithely unaware that the words might conceivably apply to himself, "to heighten the elegance of the later scenes. I'm told these Centaurs were a drunken, lustful sort. Animal passions. Course, they *were* half animals, after all. Yes, we must open with that." He fixed Anthony with an aggressive eye. "Best make a note. Antimasque of Centaurs."

Mr Challenor got a word in at last. "Centaurs do not appear in the stories of Pegasus," he said crushingly.

"Then we'll put 'em in. Make a most effective scene. They were half horses, weren't they?"

"I can't possibly agree to this! My reputation as a scholar!"

"We're putting on an entertainment, not writing a learned book."

"*I* am writing a poetic drama. Your business, Mr Huntley, is to stage it – to do whatever is necessary," said Mr Challenor, "to translate my verses into simulated reality. The costumes, the scenery, the mechanical devices . . . You will have enough to do, if the performance is to equal the conception of my fantasy."

"Well, we shall have to see, shan't we?" said the designer ominously.

They continued for another hour. Anthony made a number of notes but was not clear at the end just what had been agreed. If anything.

97

Nine *A Curse on Crucorney*

The return to Crucorney was slightly more leisurely, for Ravenwood travelled with a considerable cavalcade.

In those weeks away the spring had unrolled a vast carpet of green and white and coral pink over the western midlands. They found the Priory embowered in fruit-blossom. The river, bustling along beneath the high garden wall, was no longer a winter torrent but a good-humoured, almost playful stream.

On its far side the new castle buildings lined the wooded heights. The long ranks of windows now winked with glass. The bare bones of the roof-beams were fleshed with tiles where they were not covered with lead. Pausing only to embrace his wife and children, the impulsive Ravenwood insisted that they mount fresh horses and inspect the site before supper.

At close quarters the progress was even more impressive. The Banqueting Hall and Great Gallery were practically finished. Though much of the fine interior work would never be completed by the end of the summer, the bareness could be softened with tapestries and hangings. In the Little Castle skilled craftsmen swarmed like ants, painting panels and bosses, gilding star-spangled ceilings, laying black and white marble floors, and installing ornate chimneypieces of Italian and Turkish design.

Ravenwood, now fully recovered from his wound, ran up and down the staircases and strode briskly round the courtyard, stopping only to question the workmen or to congratulate them on their efforts.

The superb stable-block was near completion, with its own forge and harness-rooms. Next to it, tall double doors stood open to the Riding House. From the spectators' gallery they looked down admiringly into the echoing interior, under the tremendous hammer-beams of Crucorney oak.

"It's a hundred feet by thirty-three," his lordship told them proudly. "Space enough to show His Majesty what my horses can do!" He would have the gallery hung with cloth-of-gold, and two chairs of state provided for his royal guests. He talked exuberantly as though their coming was already assured.

Back at the Priory, there was just time to wash away the stains of travel and put on fresh linen before they were called to supper. As before, Anthony found himself bidden to eat with the family, and was not relegated to the parlour with the chief officers of the household. He could only hope that there would be no jealousy. He seemed to be accepted here not just as Mandeville's secretary but as a guest, however young and lowly, in his own right. That was typical of my lord's courtesy.

He sat quiet while Lady Ravenwood and her husband exchanged their news. "The men have worked splendidly," his lordship declared warmly.

"Long may they continue." Anthony wondered if he caught, in her tone, the merest hesitancy.

"Why should they not?"

She glanced round. The servants had removed the main dishes. She waited while they set fruit and more wine upon the table, and trimmed the candles. Then, as the door closed behind them, she burst out as though the words had been too long bottled within her: "You never told me there was a ghost at Crucorney!"

Ravenwood's jaw dropped. "A ghost? My dear Rose,

I never heard of one."

Anthony stopped eating and studied their faces. Despite his lordship's reassuring answer, the word had sent a disconcerting chill down his own spine. Except in childhood, the thought of ghosts had seldom troubled him. In workaday London they seemed not to be part of people's ordinary experience. But here, in this wild mountain region on the fringe of Wales, eerie things were still said to happen. Spells and witchcraft lingered. Tobias had told him so. Perhaps ghosts walked?

"I was afraid you had been keeping it from me," said her ladyship with obvious relief.

"I grew up in this house. I have never heard the least whisper of such a thing. Has anyone seen it?"

"That's what I can't find out. It started with some talk among the workmen. Not our own people. The masons from Hereford, I think. But no one will admit to anything."

"And where is this spectre supposed to have shown itself?"

"In this house. A monkish figure. Hooded." Lady Ravenwood had questioned the steward, who in turn had examined all the household servants. None of them had admitted to seeing anything unusual. But many had heard the gossip going round outside.

Mandeville broke in. "If the story concerns the Priory, what is it to do with the masons up at the castle?"

"There's some notion of a curse on the whole venture – and all who take part in it."

"A curse?" Ravenwood looked as incredulous as before.

His wife recounted the story as far as she had managed to piece it together. It was now almost a hundred years since the monks had been expelled and the house sold to the then Lord Ravenwood. One monk – some said it was the Prior – had bitterly denounced the new occupant. Very well, he had declared, make your home if you wish in what is rightly God's house and ours. But if, after turning us out, the Ravenwoods ever abandon this place for another, then a curse on them and all who serve them in the enterprise.

"Some say," she concluded, "that the monk has been seen in the last week or two. And that a ghostly voice has been heard in the night, repeating the curse."

Ravenwood burst out laughing. Anthony found that hearty sound comforting, but not completely so. "Someone, dear Rose, has been reading old plays. *Hamlet*, perhaps. After too heavy a supper."

"It may not be a laughing matter," said Mandeville gently.

"Renold! Don't tell me you believe this bugaboo nonsense?"

Mandeville ignored the question. "The workmen may. And you want no interruptions."

"I won't have them! I'll have the place ready if they have to work on by lantern-light."

"They may not relish *that*. In the circumstances."

"There will be double pay. Money speaks louder than monks – especially monks who've not been seen for a hundred years. This tale – this legend – call it what you will – I have never heard a word of it in all my life before." He turned and fixed an unusually stern look upon his wife. "And remember, Rose, *I* have known this house since I toddled round it in my uncle's time. *You* never saw it till I brought you here as my bride." Lady Ravenwood wilted at this implied reproof. Anthony, who had come to admire her, and her beauty, with a distant devotion, was sorry to see her so put down.

This seemed to close the subject. "I have a dozen more practical difficulties to worry my head with," said his lordship. And, well aware that he had, the others refrained from continuing the argument.

No supernatural manifestations disturbed the night that followed. Even Anthony, though he said his prayers with more than usual diligence, enjoyed the sound sleep of any healthy youth who had spent a long day in the saddle. But he was not sorry when Mandeville announced next morning that they would push straight on to Wildhope. There was the matter of Amoret's visit, and the sooner he faced his mother the better.

Arrived at Wildhope, they found her bluffly welcoming as ever, full of impatient exclamations at having grand guests wished upon her at so busy a season, yet pleased with herself that all the preparations were ordered in good time.

"I have had the west wing made ready for the Grisedales. It will be good to have it used again. The young lord in the blue chamber, his sister and her maid at the far end."

"I thought we might give her the great chamber. I shall be happy to move to the room I had as a boy."

"Most unsuitable." Lady Mandeville's lips met in a hard little line. "The great chamber is for the master of Wildhope. No girl will sleep there. Except as your bride."

Mandeville shrugged his shoulders. Clearly he did not want another discussion on that matter.

Over dinner, she demanded the latest news of Ravenwood and his extravagant follies. Anthony was a little surprised that Mandeville told her about a rumour of a ghost. Then he remembered that she was a mine of information on this whole neighbourhood, and her son turned naturally to her for information.

"Crucorney poke-ridden?" she exclaimed. "That's news indeed. But I would believe anything of Crucorney. They say young Will has everything, so I suppose he must even have his own ghost."

Mandeville mentioned the monk's curse. "You have never heard of it, Mother?"

She shook her head vigorously. "Never! And I trust the notion will not spread. Even Wildhope took its cut of the old monastery lands. The rough grazing on Pendock Hill belonged once to the monks of Crucorney." She gave a little cackling laugh. "I want no hooded apparitions up there, frightening our ewes and making them drop their lambs!"

"I fancy we shan't be troubled here," said Mandeville with a thoughtful look.

"The monks were enough nuisance while they lived. They were pensioned off. The new landlords had to carry the cost of their pensions," said her ladyship grimly, "and I believe the monks were a long-lived lot."

"In no hurry to become ghosts, madam?" Anthony ventured a feeble jest, and was rewarded with a smile.

"Certainly not, Mr Bassey. So they need not start now!"

It was evident that any monk returning now to walk the upland pastures would meet with a discouraging reception from Lady Mandeville.

Gradually, Anthony told himself hopefully, he was being accepted by this intimidating woman. He would never overcome certain handicaps in her eyes – that he was a townsman, a Londoner, and half Italian. But as Mandeville had taken him into service, she seemed to recognise that things could have been worse. She knew he was loyal and dependable. She had begun to realise that sometimes she might achieve more by a tactful word to him than by a stand-up argument with her son.

On the second day she seized a chance to draw Anthony apart. Casually – but quite unconvincingly – she turned the conversation to the Grisedales.

"This young Lord Grisedale... Has my son known him long?"

Not knowing how much Mandeville had told her, Anthony could only be evasive.

"I am not sure, madam. When Sir Renold is in town

he goes to many houses – and sometimes to court, of course. He does not tell me of all the gentlemen he meets."

"Naturally not. In any case, I understand that his lordship is only a boy. He will not yet have taken his proper place in the world."

"I believe he is much given to riding, and country sports."

"We must do what we can to entertain him. Though my son has far too little interest in such things." Her ladyship sniffed. She had her own ideas about the occupations proper for a gentleman. "And this sister? The Honourable Amoret? Where does *she* come in?"

Where indeed, thought Anthony? He must answer as harmlessly as he could.

"She is at court, madam. A Maid of Honour."

"Ah, so that accounts for her acquaintance with Sir Renold. They met there." Lady Mandeville spoke in a well-satisfied tone, as if something at least had clicked into place. Anthony felt it more prudent not to say that in fact their meeting had chanced very differently.

"You will not have seen her yourself, Mr Bassey?"

This time it seemed safer to correct any false impression. It would be fatal when Lady Mandeville saw them together. "I did see her, madam, a fortnight or more ago. When we went with my Lord Ravenwood to Hampton Court. It was by accident in the palace gardens."

Luckily her ladyship jumped to the obvious assumption that he had been with Mandeville at the time. She hastened to put the questions uppermost in her mind.

"What is she like? Is she good-looking?"

"I would say, beautiful," said Anthony emphatically.

Lady Mandeville demanded a more detailed account. Height? Colouring? Figure? She might have been standing in a country market, appraising the points of an animal it was in her mind to bid for.

"Both parents dead. That's bad. Do you know how they died, Mr Bassey?"

"The father was killed fighting in the Low Countries – a gentleman volunteer with the Dutch. In her mother's case I believe it was the smallpox."

"Anyone can die of that," Lady Mandeville conceded generously. "So, it does not seem a weakly stock. And there are estates, it seems, both in Kent and in Derbyshire."

"So I understand, madam."

"And some of the land is settled on the young lady," said Lady Mandeville thoughtfully. "Have you any notion how much? Not the acreage. The rent-roll?"

"No, madam." Anthony assumed his most wooden face. "If Sir Renold asked, he has not told me."

"No matter. In a week or two I shall be meeting the young lady myself. I only hope," she added darkly, "I am not about to see the curse of Wildhope descend upon us, never mind Crucorney!"

Ten *Designs and Devices*

It was Fabian, of course, who boy-like insisted on their taking the steepest, highest road across the Malverns, though the guide they had engaged in Worcester warned them that they would tire the horses and have to sleep at the Feathers in Ledbury instead of reaching Hereford that night.

Amoret had agreed reluctantly, judging it better for once to let her brother have his way. He had fallen in with her suggestion of a duty visit to Derbyshire, and, tempted by the promise of a visit to Lord Ravenwood's renowned stables, he had made no objection to this roundabout return journey. So, when the guide had pointed out the towering heights ahead, and announced that the Malvern Hills were often called "the English Alps", she let the absurdity pass without argument. Better to cross this ridge than cross Fabian.

Alps, though! Her mind flew back to memories of Savoy. The high snowfields, the avalanche... It would be good to meet again the people with whom it was safe to recall those adventurous days. Fabian, of course, knew of that escapade. But even inside the family, her grandmother had decreed, it should be regarded as unmentionable, if ever Amoret was to hope for a husband of suitable rank. So, there must be no impatient, elder-sisterly cry of, "Wait till you see the real Alps!" She must gape at the guide's bidding, as though she had never seen a mountain in her life.

She had to admit, as they toiled up the long slanting ascent, these hills were for England considerable enough. The slopes of grass and shimmering bracken fell dizzily to the valley. Her maid, perched pillion behind one of the grooms, squealed constantly with dismay. Betty considered that she was being carried into a savage world of unknown perils. Even the familiar sight of hopfields and oasthouses a few miles back – the first they had seen since leaving Kent a month ago – did nothing to reconcile her to this endless travelling, further and further away from home.

When at last they reached the rocky backbone of the ridge, and slid from the saddle to give their panting beasts a well-earned pause, the new prospect before them made Fabian's whim seem amply worth while. At their feet an immense rumpled patchwork of cornfield and orchard, copse and meadow, went undulating up and down, up and down, with hillocks and humps innumerable into a smoky amethyst blue of distance. Above and beyond that fading haze more hills stood up, definite again, black against a rain-threatening western sky.

She thought of Moses, looking down upon the promised land. And for herself, too – if the Bible comparison was not irreverent – this was a kind of promised land. Somewhere at the feet of those far-off hills, another two days' ride over these appalling roads, was Mandeville.

Long days they proved. The Kentish servants vowed that two Herefordshire miles would have made three at home. But there were no misadventures, no floods or broken bridges, no highway robbers, not so much as a cast shoe. Late in the afternoon of the day she had reckoned on, they saw the head of the valley rearing green in front of them and the clustering gables of the Hall above the treetops.

Her knees felt suddenly weak, and she knew it was not only the weariness of many hours in the saddle.

She had thought so much about her first confrontation with Mandeville, she had not prepared herself for meeting his mother. But of course it was Lady Mandeville who welcomed them. Of her son, and of sympathetic dependable Anthony, there was no sign.

The ladies embraced. Fabian made a creditable bow and kissed her ladyship's useful-looking hand.

"My son should have been here to greet you," said Lady Mandeville.

He should ... oh, he should, thought Amoret. Aloud, she said, striving for the cool poise that was so much admired at court: "Indeed, no, madam! We are at fault for not sending word ahead of us. But it was hard to be sure of times and distances. It seemed best to press on and make all the speed we could."

"Of course." It seemed like an age as they stood there, appraising each other. It could only have been a moment or two, for this keen-eyed little woman, though her gown might be ten years behind the fashion, was no mannerless rustic. "You must be tired, my dear. I will show you, and his lordship, to your rooms."

Then – she had barely set foot on the stairs behind her hostess – Mandeville was there. She spun round at his voice, stumbled, and almost slipped. His hand was firm under her elbow till she had recovered her balance. Then her own gloved hand was lightly taken, and she was looking down at the dark, copper-glinting head bowed over it in a conventional kiss.

"Sir Renold!"

"Madam!"

Afterwards, she was to shake with inward laughter, remembering the formality of the meeting. She did not know how much he had told his mother of their previous acquaintance. A good deal less – she felt certain – than she had told Fabian and her grandmother. Fabian, mercifully, was well drilled in discretion. He knew that if the Mandeville visit went amiss, he would never see the inside of Lord Ravenwood's stables.

So the tricky social moment passed without mishap.

And the evening that followed. It was mainly her ladyship who steered the conversation. That was about their journey, how they had found their estates in Derbyshire, their grandmother's health, their life with her in Kent.

Lady Mandeville seemed entirely indifferent to court gossip or news from town. As for foreign countries, they barely existed. There were no awkward references that would have made it embarrassing to meet Anthony's eyes across the table. Mandeville's she did not meet at all. He had withdrawn into that enigmatic reserve she remembered so well. He was a courteous host, but, apart from pressing her to more food and drink, he addressed most of his few remarks to Fabian.

Only when they left the table and moved to another room did he single her out for a quick word.

"It is good to see you here – in this remote corner of ours – almost at the end of the world!"

She answered lightly, in the tone she had picked up from the Queen's ladies: "I would gladly go to the world's end, sir – to help a friend of yours."

He frowned – either disliking the frivolity, or so intent on his own thoughts that he ignored it. "If Lord Ravenwood is to get the King to Crucorney this year, we have got to act quickly. How soon do you go back to court?"

"As soon as I please. I can set Fabian on his road home. I need not go down to Kent myself."

"Excellent," he said. And no more. At least, no more of consequence. In the withdrawing room he seized a lute and insisted on their all joining in madrigals. It was his way, she decided, of checking his mother's flow of searching questions.

In her own room, when a yawning Betty had helped her undress, she dismissed the girl to her truckle bed.

She went along and opened her brother's door. The candle was still burning. He blinked sleepily from between the parted curtains of his bed.

"What is the matter?"

"I wanted to see your room." She meant Mandeville's – the room that had been his as a boy. She glanced round, but of course it told her nothing. It was like any room.

"How long must we stay here?" Fabian demanded.

"Not long, I think. Why?"

"She wants to know so much—"

"Sh!"

"I like Sir Renold. And you do, don't you?"

"Certainly."

"The way you were looking at him. When we were all singing." Fabian was wide awake now. Far too wide awake, she thought.

"I must get some sleep," she said, moving towards the door.

"I would not mind your marrying him," said Fabian generously. "He is only a baronet, but still—"

"You would be happier with a brother-in-law of lower rank than yourself!" she retorted acidly.

"So long as he was well-born. Not like this Bassey fellow. I noticed the way *he* was looking at *you*."

"Stop talking such nonsense! And don't dare to speak like that of Anthony. He's—" She stopped. Vexed and confused, she could not find the words to say what Anthony was. "I have not even thought of marrying anyone," she said with dignity.

"You'll have to, sooner or later. All girls do." He snuffed out the candle, leaving her to grope her way through the door. The last she heard of him was his insufferable chuckling from behind his curtains.

It seemed to suit everyone that their stay at Wildhope should not be long. Fabian was itching to reach Crucorney. There were no fine riding horses here – it was a vast farm Lady Mandeville was managing, he declared disgustedly, not a gentleman's estate – and in any case this was too rough and breakneck a country for good sport. Mandeville was equally restive, and she guessed that it was not only the urgency of Lord Ravenwood's business – she could see, and sympathise with, his irritation at his mother's far from subtle tactics.

Even Lady Mandeville, having now satisfied her curiosity, did not press her guests to linger indefinitely. She had found out the Grisedale pedigree on both sides and had assured herself that they were a healthy breeding stock. She had looked Amoret up and down, commented frankly on her too boyish slimness, but consoled her with the assurance that in due course child-bearing would take care of that. She had almost certainly, Amoret told herself, estimated the value of the Derbyshire dowry more accurately than the Grisedales themselves had. With her son displaying no sign of interest, there was not much more that she could do for the present, though she told Amoret darkly, "I shall, of course, be writing to your grandmother. It is only civil, after the pleasure of entertaining you."

Amoret rode away from Wildhope less inclined towards marriage than she had ever been. Had she been a green girl, cherishing those old romantic recollections of Mandeville? Where was the fascinating cavalier, the dare-devil, Mad Mandeville? As for marriage – to anyone – no! For a girl it was not a question of love but of legal settlements, drawn up by families. And then – she shuddered – babies year after year in wearisome succession, half of them destined for the churchyard without ever growing up to know the full wonder of life.

Life *was* wonderful, she still felt that. The old zest returned as they rode over the windy skyline. Crucorney lay ahead, fresh people, the fascinating project of the masque, and above all the challenging problem, how to persuade the King and Queen . . .

Yes, she might have little else in common with the courtiers she had mixed with in the past few months – even less perhaps with Lady Mandeville – but she was beginning to understand their pleasure in manipulation and intrigue.

Mandeville, having devoted his attention to Fabian for the first mile, dropped back to ride beside her. "You must not mind my mother," he said in a low voice.

She made no direct answer to that, but she felt a little thrill of pleasure at his tone. Now that they were clear of Wildhope, the old easy relationship was back. Liberation was in the air. She could speak more naturally to Anthony. She had even received a most disrespectful but friendly wink from Tobias Fludd.

"I am looking forward to Crucorney," she said. "To meet Lord Ravenwood – to hear more about the masque—"

"You'll hear plenty of that! The designer should have arrived from London. We may meet our poet, too."

"The more I know, the more chance I have of working on their Majesties."

He questioned her about her life at court. It was not idle curiosity – he was treating her now as a young woman, giving her credit for shrewd observation, valuing her opportunities for inside knowledge.

"I think you are right about the Marquis of Lockerbie," she said. "Of all the men close to the King he best fills the bill. He's a climber, but he's not sure of his own foothold yet."

"And I think *you* are right about the Queen – win her goodwill, and we're halfway to winning the King's."

"Oh, he doesn't agree with her always—"

"Thank God for that! I suspect that her political judgement is even worse than his. But in a small matter like this, whether or not they should visit Crucorney – that's where her wishes might just tip the scale. So, anything you can do . . ."

"I'll do all I can," she promised soberly. "I do not know much about government and public matters – women are not encouraged to! But I'm not blind, or deaf. I think your friend is probably right. There are many things that are bad and wrong. Men like him are needed round the King."

A few hours later she felt doubly sure of that.

She took to Ravenwood instinctively. It was not just his youthful good looks, his athletic appearance. He was so different from the noblemen with whom she had been mixing of late. She liked his frankness, his warmth, so unlike the reserve and the smooth-tongued insincerity of the court. She liked the way he treated everyone, young and old, high and low, with the same natural civility – Fabian or Anthony or this rough-edged theatrical mechanic, Huntley. He listened, as well as talked, to them.

Here is a man, she thought, who could straddle that wide perilous gap between the King and the common people.

Not least she liked the way he treated her. Not – as this poet, Challenor, was doing – as a merely ornamental young lady, whose opinions were not to be taken seriously, but who must be fed with artificial compliments as a lap-dog was plied with titbits. Ravenwood paid her the only compliment she ever wanted: he gave her credit for possessing intelligence.

After dinner, of course, they must all go across to the new castle. She rode in the coach with Lady Ravenwood and the children, glad of the chance to make their closer acquaintance and not begrudging Fabian the undivided attention of their host. At all costs Fabian must be kept happy if their visit was to go well.

The signs for that were promising. Her brother had been mounted on a splendid light bay Spanish mare and offered a wide choice of other horses to try tomorrow.

And by the time the lumbering coach had reached the castle courtyard and disgorged its passengers, the gentlemen had admired the stables and were up in the spectators' gallery of the Riding House. Only Mr Challenor and Huntley stood outside, a little sulkily, because this part of the visit had no interest for them. They did not even have the consolation of each other's conversation. She had noticed at dinner that, though they were collaborators in the project of the masque, they seldom exchanged a remark.

A brief glimpse of these buildings was enough for Amoret. The Riding House had its own vast magnificence, but it was bare and plain. She was eager to go into the more elegant apartments ranged round the other sides of the court, and that fairy-tale Little Castle of which she had caught a distant glimpse through the coach window.

"And now," her host exclaimed clapping his hands, "the Great Gallery – and the Banqueting Hall!"

He started off briskly, the ladies swishing behind him in their long skirts, the gentlemen bringing up the rear, while Margaret and Gilbert raced free like puppies.

Within the past year Amoret had seen several palaces. The court had been to Windsor and Greenwich and Richmond, as well as Hampton and Whitehall. She was no longer staggered by size and splendour. But all the royal homes were old. Never had she seen a comparable building rising fresh from its foundations.

Mr Challenor had attached himself to her, murmuring attentively in his affected drawl. "What do you think of it all?"

"Superb," she said with complete sincerity.

"I agree. And the prospects in every direction – Arcadian! Crucorney will be a jewel in a perfect setting. My Muse responds! Which is fortunate," he added bitterly.

"I imagined your poem was already written?"

"It was. But this fellow—" He paused cautiously and

114

glanced down the Banqueting Hall. Huntley was safely out of earshot, scribbling in a notebook. "His notions require so many changes. New scenes that have nothing to do with the story. All so that he may show off his ingenious devices. He has got round his lordship – he is to have his way, and I must compose new verses to go with them. Though who will heed my verses, when they are all gaping at his floating clouds and flying goddesses—" He shrugged his shoulders.

Amoret felt a sneaking sympathy for him. "The King will," she said soothingly. "The King has a taste for poetry – he loves Shakespeare. It is the Queen's poor grasp of English – that is why the stage effects are so important. And the music, and the dancing, the costumes and the lights. But there could be no masque unless the poet came first."

"You hearten me, dear lady. I treasure your encouragement."

What you truly mean, thought Amoret, is that you are very mindful I am a Maid of Honour. In our little party this afternoon I am the only courtier. The one person, besides of course his opulent lordship, whose friendship could be useful.

They passed on, and the workmen were allowed to resume their hammering.

The Banqueting Hall, she learned, was to be used for the masque itself, not for the banquet preceding it. That was the masterful Huntley again. He insisted that only the Banqueting Hall was high enough to leave space for his loft above the stage. He needed the loft to accommodate the pulleys and winches and other equipment for the manipulation of scenery and effects. People could eat anywhere. So, given settled weather, the feast could be set out along the terrace or perhaps in the garden enclosed within the remnants of the ancient ramparts. And if rain threatened, the Great Gallery would serve.

Amoret was becoming a little intrigued by this man

who, despite his lowly birth and uncultivated manner, seemed to have cast so powerful a spell upon his aristocratic patron. She would not be prejudiced either by his appearance or by Challenor's sneers. She admired independence. Huntley certainly had that.

It was not until after supper that she had the chance to speak more than a word to him. Then Lord Ravenwood suggested that he show her some of the rough sketches he had made for the costumes and scenery. Huntley's eyes narrowed suspiciously, as if to question what business it was of hers, but Ravenwood added a discreet reminder that this was the young lady who might enlist the Queen's interest.

Huntley saw the point of that. His sketches, he growled, were in the long gallery. A better place to see them, he made clear, than here amid the chatter round the table, where wine might be spilt upon them.

"I will come to the gallery then." She stood up, and at a nod from Mandeville Anthony rose to escort her.

Huntley led the way up the old oak staircase, by now all a-glimmer with candlelight. He marched heavy-footed and confident, though he had been a guest in the Priory only since the previous day. The house might have been his own.

The gallery was even dimmer. "Best bring over that other candlestick," he told Anthony, and Anthony meekly brought the extra lights to the table in a window-bay where the designer was already spreading out his sketches.

Amoret caught her breath.

It was incredible that those work-worn fingers could have wielded a pencil with such exquisite delicacy. That from under this bald brown pate, with its scruffy fringe of red hair, such fantastically beautiful conceptions could emerge.

"Here—" He laid a sketch of wild mountain landscape before her. "Here we have Mount Olympus. When the scene parts, the mountain opens to show this—" A Greek temple was placed over the first drawing. "Perseus comes down out of the clouds, flying with his magic winged sandals. Then, when the thunder peals, I have devised this other transformation—"

Yet the most remarkable transformation, she thought, was in this homely Worcestershire mechanic himself. Expounding his ideas he lost his brusqueness. He was a man inspired.

"It will be most wonderful," she said huskily.

"These are mere scribblings!"

"But I can imagine how it will look when finished. These mountains – the woods – the waterfall—" She remembered what Challenor had said about the stimulus of the scenery round Crucorney. Unguardedly, she asked if it had influenced his designs. In a moment he was his former prickly self.

"I drew these in London. I was never in this country until yesterday. Never!"

She was relieved when Anthony swiftly broke in, marvelling that Perseus was to descend out of the sky.

"That is nothing, young man. There will be other flying scenes. In the grand climax I have a dance of shadows – a saraband is the most fitting measure – and I shall contrive the moon suddenly coming out of the clouds, making the whole scene bright silver, and Bellerophon riding Pegasus across the sky—"

"Marvellous!"

"It is easy, with ropes and pulleys and counterweights. It is all worked out here in the designs." He tapped another sheaf of papers. "But you would not understand. You are not engineers. And such matters are the secrets of my craft. The costumes, though—"

With a careless gesture he took more sheets, and fanned them out across the table. Some were tinted with colours. Amoret was entranced as he gabbled the names of the characters and the costumes he planned for them.

"This will be in orange-tawny ... this will be satin, sea-green, and this aurora colour ... for this I have chosen carnation cloth of silver ... cloth of silver for this, too, but watchet blue, chevroned all over with lace..."

This man's friendship must be cultivated, she resolved. If all went well and their Majesties came to the masque, some of the court ladies would be sure to take part in the performance. Amoret Grisedale would be one of them. Amoret Grisedale must have colours that suited her.

She could have listened to Huntley's explanations half the night, but abruptly he stopped and shuffled all his sketches together again. "I'm for my bed now. I do not keep late hours as you grand folks do." They thanked him, and said good-night at the head of the stairs.

"We had better go back to the others," said Anthony wistfully.

But, like him, she was in no haste. It was a chance to exchange a few private words together. So, having descended, they lingered before rejoining the party at the table.

"Well?" he said.

"Well," she said contentedly. "This is a happy house."

"We seem to be launched on another adventure together – though hardly as full of danger this time."

"Hardly."

She laughed. And it was just then, because her face was tilted up to meet his eyes, that she was aware – behind and above him – of a movement at the turn of the stairs.

The laughter died on her lips. She could not help herself – she let out a scream and clutched at him instinctively. But when he cried out for explanation, and she lifted her cowering head to look up the stairs again, the pallid face staring from its cowl had vanished. Only a grey shadow flitted behind the carved balusters, and in a moment that too was gone.

Eleven *A Figure in Grey*

Anthony was himself just in time to catch a glimpse of the apparition vanishing upstairs. The next instant he heard another scream, not from Amoret but from somewhere above them.

It was followed by a crash, and then by peal after peal of demoniac laughter.

"My god," he gasped, unnerved. Then, making a desperate effort to control his fear, he broke free from the girl and went bounding up the stairs.

"*No!*" begged Amoret.

He took no notice. The laughter continued. At the turn of the stairs he met liquid slowly dripping down, splashing softly from one tread to the next. Blood or water? Impossible to tell in that dim light, and he shrank from testing it with his hand. And, with that unending eerie cackle just above, he could not stop for other investigations.

He reached the wide landing. A shape sprawled heaving across the lower stairs of the next flight. It was from here that the laughter came. As he rushed across, his foot encountered something which went rolling and bumping away. It was a wooden pail – a part of his mind took in that fact as he reached the fallen figure and recognised one of the maid-servants. He bent over her rather helplessly, wondering how to stop this terrible sound, when an arm reached from behind him and with a smart slap brought immediate silence.

"Hysteria," said Amoret, her own voice shaky.

The maid sat up, gasping, and in a few moments was able to stammer out her story. Coming downstairs she had seen the ghostly monk. He had glided away into the gallery.

Afterwards, Anthony wondered at the show of courage he must somehow have displayed. Inwardly he was tense with terror, but something else forced him on – shame, or perhaps the sheer instinct of pursuit. Leaving Amoret to comfort the maid, he stepped warily through the doorway into the gallery. He realised that his rapier was in his hand, though he could not remember drawing it. What use it would be against a spirit, he did not pause to consider.

The Priory gallery was of modest length compared with the palatial apartment at the castle. But it looked forbidding enough, stretching away into a gloomy distance pricked only by candles at intervals. Most ominous were the three bays, running back out of sight into even denser shadow.

He had no chance, though, to worry about what might lurk in those unseen recesses. Down the middle of the gallery a sombre figure was approaching.

A desperate prayer formed silently on his lips. He stood still, unable to drive himself another step forward. Then, in a voice shaky with relief, he said: "Mr Huntley!"

"Who did you think it was? Why are you coming at me with your sword drawn?"

The designer came forward into a little pool of candle-light. His broad collar, though none too clean, shone whitely enough above his russet coat. At close quarters he could not be mistaken, even in the most distracted fancy, for a spectral monk.

"How did *you* get here?" Anthony demanded.

That was no way to talk to Huntley. "I am not to be questioned by you, young man!"

There was a babble of excited voices in the doorway. Ravenwood, Mandeville, Fabian ... A throng of servants ... They crowded into the gallery, Amoret among them.

"Huntley!" cried his lordship. "Have *you* seen anything?"

The designer was more willing to answer him. No, he had seen nobody – until this excitable youth assailed him. He had come back to the gallery for a missing sketch which might have fallen under the table. He had entered from the far end because the backstairs provided an equally convenient way down from his chamber.

"Then whoever it is must still be here," said Ravenwood. "There are only the two doors to this gallery. No mortal man could slip out unseen." He glanced round him. "Guard both doors. I want every corner searched. Come on," he said impatiently, but the men still hesitated.

"Beg pardon, my lord," said one, "but what if it *wasn't* a mortal man?"

"If it wasn't," said his lordship, "it will have melted through the walls and won't still be here, anyhow. So what are you afraid of?"

The servants, thought Anthony, might be unconvinced by his logic but he was their master, and they all joined in a thorough search of the gallery, poking into every dark nook, opening the lid of every chest, and drawing aside each tapestry.

They found nothing.

Except Huntley, who called out that he had found his missing design beneath the table. When at last they all filed out of the gallery, only his face bore a satisfied expression. Quite unmoved by the uproar, which he put down to the fanciful imaginings of young females (a remark which won him a black glare from Amoret), he stuck to his original intention of retiring to bed.

No one else felt like doing so. They returned to the

supper-table, where Lady Ravenwood rejoined them after pacifying the hysterical maid and making sure that her children had not been awakened.

Amoret repeated her story. Anthony confirmed it, but hers was the more impressive evidence. She and Fabian had not previously heard a word of the legend, so there was no reason why she should imagine a monkish figure.

"We have been trying to prevent unnecessary alarms," said Lady Ravenwood apologetically. "It could make for all kinds of trouble."

"Up at the castle," her husband explained. "There's been a lot of idle gossip among the workmen. This story of a curse, you understand. Last week a whole gang of them stopped work for a day. But in the end I talked them round."

"Which is why the ghost walked tonight," said Mandeville quietly. "Mere rumour having failed, the spectre must be seen."

"I have ordered the servants not to say a word—"

"My dear Will," Lady Ravenwood interrupted, "you know the story will be all over the neighbourhood tomorrow. You might as well try to stop that river flowing past outside!"

"I do not understand, my lord," said Challenor. "Does someone wish to obstruct your building plans? But who? And why?"

"It is possible. You know the world, Mr Challenor. You know its jealousies. But I name no names." His lordship could curb his tongue when it was desirable.

"Do *you* believe in ghosts, Mr Challenor?" Lady Ravenwood deftly steered the conversation away to a more general question.

"My reason says no, madam, but I admit I am shaken."

There was a lively discussion now on the supernatural. No one was positive that ghosts and evil spirits did not exist – Anthony could see that Lady Ravenwood was particularly uneasy, and he felt some sympathy with her.

He had seen the apparition too briefly to be sure whether it had been an insubstantial spectre or a man dressed up. The maid testified that it had disappeared into the gallery. There could not have been time for anyone to escape through the other door without being seen by Huntley. As to the obvious suggestion, that there was a third, concealed exit, Ravenwood scoffed at it. If there had been, he would have known of it. His father would have told him before he died.

"Nevertheless," said Mandeville, "and whether ghosts exist or do not, I will not accept this one. He comes altogether too pat on cue, like Hamlet's father, just when the plot requires him. There's a natural explanation. We shall find it. We must. Quickly."

That was no exaggeration. As Lady Ravenwood had foreseen, there was no way to stop news of the event spreading first through the household and thence leaking to the world outside. By noon, fearsomely adorned with grisly additions, it was being discussed all over the building site. There was unanimous agreement that, whatever the pressure, whatever the pay my lord offered, no one would work after sunset. This affected only a small number of craftsmen engaged on urgent jobs, and in any case with the lengthening evenings was not as serious as it would have been a month or two earlier. But there were also some men who declared that they would not work there a day longer, demanded their money, and decamped.

At supper Lord Ravenwood's usual urbanity was absent. His brow was furrowed with private thoughts as the conversation ran dispiritedly round the table.

On one point all agreed: if the apparent phantom were indeed, as Mandeville insisted, some malicious living person, he could hardly be a member of the Priory household, all of whom had been with the family for years and were completely trusted. It was equally unthinkable that he was in the Grisedale party, all complete strangers from the other side of England, who had arrived only a few hours previously and whose visit to Crucorney had been a private arrangement unknown to most of them beforehand.

So, if it had been mere play-acting, the actor had been someone else with no right to be in the house.

"He shan't slip in again," said his lordship grimly.

Fortunately, though the Priory was large and rambling, it was not difficult to make proof against intruders. When adapted as a private dwelling it had kept the high wall which had encircled the original monastery precincts. On the garden side, too, there was the extra defence of the river rushing past outside. Once the great gate was barred for the night, and the rear gate also, the Priory became a little castle in itself.

There was always a watchman in case of fire. Now, for the present, he should have two companions to keep up his spirits and strengthen the patrolling during the dark hours. They would have dogs, and there would be another dog running free in the garden.

At Mandeville's suggestion, Ravenwood's own favourite hound, Bellman, would henceforth sleep at the door of the great chamber. "I would not alarm Rose," Mandeville murmured when her ladyship was out of earshot, "but suppose – I don't know how – these other precautions fail? Our ghostly friend merely came out on the staircase and made a wench drop her pail. He could as well have caught *you* – and fired a pistol. After all, that was how the whole business began."

"True, Renold. I'll take every care."

There were no alarms that night. It was not until his lordship had taken his morning ride and breakfasted that he went to his study for a book he had promised Challenor.

The room was in disorder. Anthony saw it himself, before it was tidied. Papers strewed the floor, books were scattered in heaps. Not surprisingly, no servant could explain it. No one had entered the room since the previous day.

There was no damage. Nothing appeared to be missing. In any case, Ravenwood insisted, the papers were neither secret nor important. They concerned petty estate matters, accounts and bills, the pedigrees of his best horses, personal letters from distant relatives and friends.

"We have a mischievous sprite," said Mandeville, stroking his moustache thoughtfully. "He wishes us to know that he is still around."

The actual disturbance of the study was nothing to the mental turmoil into which Crucorney was now thrown.

All the careful precautions had been shown to be useless. Patrolling dogs and men, locked gates and doors, and a close observation of every outsider entering and leaving the premises by day, had failed to keep out the mysterious visitant.

Opinion naturally swung towards the daunting theory of a genuine ghost. Mandeville and Ravenwood stood almost alone as confident unbelievers. Anthony himself swayed this way and that, unhappily, afraid that for once his master was mistaken.

Up at the castle the work went on. But so did the uneasy murmuring. A few more of the Hereford craftsmen took themselves off, and among the estate workers there was a sudden increase of illness most unusual at that season of the year. Some said the absences were due to fear. Others argued that the sicknesses were real, and that the monk's curse was beginning to take effect. One man, as he was paid off and took his departure, prophesied that the next thing would be an outbreak of plague.

Three days and nights went by without further alarms. Amoret and her brother, to the considerable relief of their servants, set out for London. She promised to give the Queen a tempting description of the new castle and the projected masque. But her expression was clouded as she said goodbye to Anthony. "I only hope that everything will be ready in time," she murmured. "And that somehow this ghost – or whatever it proves to be – will be laid to rest before then." It was a weighty responsibility, he could imagine, to persuade their Majesties to come to Crucorney.

Mr Challenor had hoped to travel with the Grisedale party, but Huntley's constant flow of new ideas, demanding the rewriting of this scene, the omission of that, and the substitution of some completely new speeches to match his stage-effects, meant that he had to stay and fight to save the tattered remains of his original script. The continual bickering of the two men at least provided some comic relief from the heavier anxieties.

It was on the night after Amoret's departure that Anthony, who normally enjoyed the sound sleep of healthy youth, was awakened by the brightness of the moonlight falling upon his face. He sat up, wishing he had bed-curtains like Mandeville in the next room, but thankful that his low truckle bed could easily be trundled across the floor into the shadows. He only half believed the old wives' tale that, if you slept with the moon on your face, you would go mad. But at this witching hour, in this house that might or might not be haunted, he was not inclined to take chances. He got out of bed, pushed it well out of the slanting moonbeam, and, before getting in again, took a look out of the window.

The courtyard lay below, pale as cheese. Bright as it was, a bobbing twinkle showed that the watchmen were not to be parted from their lantern. It was good to see them, two stolid figures stumping across the yard, a dog padding silent at their heels. He turned away, cheered by the sight, and at that moment a voice pealed out across the stillness.

He sprang back to the window, thrust the casement wider open, and craned out. The voice came from overhead – out of the sky, it might have been, and sure enough the watchmen were staring up at some point high above him. He had not caught the words spoken, but now, with his head stuck out, he heard the voice plainly. "Take heed—" the second word was drawn out in a manner that chilled the blood. "A curse on all who build a new Crucorney!"

The words died on the air. The watchmen came suddenly to life. Shouting, they raced towards the house, the dog barking excitedly.

Anthony ran to rouse Mandeville. "It would be upstairs," he stammered. "Perhaps even on the roof." Pausing only to pull on breeches and boots, they seized their rapiers and clattered up to the top floor.

Above and below them the entire household was in mounting uproar. Amid such a babble of question and answer, such a confused flicker of hastily kindled lights, such a banging of doors and colliding of persons, and Bellman racing to and fro, any orderly search was impossible. Despairingly, his lordship ordered everyone back to bed except his guests and a handful of his most stalwart men.

The two watchmen swore that they had seen the monk as clear as if it had been daylight. He had stood on the roof, outlined against a drifting cloud, a figure in a grey habit, arms upstretched in a terrible gesture of denunciation. And from the shadow of the hood concealing his face had come that ringing voice, pronouncing the curse that was now common knowledge.

Anthony joined the party that searched the roof. It was a somewhat giddy business, filing round the leads, steadying oneself against chimneystacks,. with the stone parapet so low and the paved courtyard so far beneath. Not surprisingly, they found no trace of the spectral figure.

There seemed no point in going back to bed. The sky was already whitening above the eastward hills. His lordship called for wine and something to eat. "We shall see no more tonight," he said.

"Nor today, I fancy," said Mandeville. "Our fox will run to ground for a while, till he knows the result of his latest effort."

"Which will be considerable, I'm afraid, now that the rogue has been heard as well as seen. Those words will be quoted everywhere." Ravenwood sounded more dejected than Anthony had ever known him.

In spite of the watchmen outside and the prompt rousing of the household, they had neither prevented the manifestation nor come any nearer catching the perpetrator. Whoever had been on the roof could have stripped off his grey robe in a moment and mingled with the excited household unrecognised.

"By the way," said Mandeville, "where is our friend Huntley?"

No one had seen the designer. "Doubtless," drawled Challenor, "he has slept soundly throughout the business."

"We mustn't begrudge him," said Ravenwood. "He works all hours on his devices. Pray God it won't all be wasted."

Mandeville jumped up from the table with an air of sudden decision, draining his glass. "I am going to finish dressing," he told Anthony. "Find Tobias. Tell him to get our horses saddled."

Ravenwood stared. "Where—?" he began. He was one of the few who dared question Mandeville.

Mandeville clowned, putting on a comical child's expression. "I don't like haunted houses," he wailed. "I am going home to my mother." They all laughed. It relieved the tension. As Anthony reached the door, Mandeville called: "No need for you to come. We shall ride hard. If my mother is not out bullying the tenants I can speak with her and be back by dusk."

What idea had seized him he did not divulge. But he had been gone barely an hour when Anthony, thinking of Lady Mandeville at her table strewn with estate accounts, was struck by an idea of his own. He sought out his lordship.

"By all means, Anthony! It can do no harm. It might reassure my wife. Though I fear any amount of musty documents won't satisfy the workmen."

Armed with this permission, Anthony spent a dusty morning in the muniment room, sorting through records that went back a century. His lordship's secretary was at first puzzled, then equally keen on the scent. With his help, Anthony was able to summarise the relevant facts on a single sheet of paper.

When the Crucorney monastery was dissolved in 1536 it had already been in a state of decay. Numbers had dwindled, as in many other religious houses, and there were only six monks left, two of them very old. The closure had been accepted without any of the resistance shown in some parts of the country. The prior, the sub-prior and the other four brothers had accepted pensions, and those who wished to remain in the neighbourhood had been provided with cottages by the Lord Ravenwood of those days. One of them had become a parish priest. Another had eventually renounced his vows, married and fathered a family.

The estate records had all their names and the years of their deaths, when each pension terminated. There was no evidence of resentment, much less of any dramatic cursing. If any such scene had taken place, Lord Ravenwood would scarcely have continued to pay each pension so regularly.

The results of Anthony's research did something to cheer an otherwise depressed party at the dinner-table. Her ladyship, who had been much shaken by the events of the night, was more prepared now to accept her husband's assurances. He vowed that the legend of the curse was a new fabrication, just as the apparition was mere trickery. Challenor stoutly supported him.

"Such effects are easy to contrive, madam." His lip curled as he glanced across the table at Huntley. "I am sure our ingenious friend here could conjure up a thousand devils for you." The designer glowered at the sneer, but said nothing.

The trouble was, as Ravenwood had said, old papers carried little weight with superstitious workmen, whereas the hair-raising report of last night's excitement did. Before dinner was over a distracted foreman brought news that all work had stopped for the day. The men were debating whether to start again tomorrow. They were being stirred up by trouble-makers.

"Devil take them!" cried his lordship. "They deserve whipping. And if I could just lay my hands on the fellow who is playing the ghost—" Words failed him. His genial humour was fast fraying to shreds.

The table broke up. Challenor plucked his sleeve. "If I might have a word in private, my lord?" He turned to detain Anthony as he was following the others from the room. "I would like Mr Bassey to stay."

"By all means." Ravenwood looked puzzled. "You had better close the door, Anthony. Well, Mr Challenor?"

The poet cleared his throat and seemed embarrassed. "I am sure you are right, my lord, that we are dealing with no supernatural spirit. It is some malicious trickster. Your lordship is equally confident it is no member of your household—"

"I'd stake my life on their loyalty. All of them!"

"That narrows the field. You have sealed the house against intruders. And so—"

It was Ravenwood who now looked troubled. "What are you suggesting, Mr Challenor? Whom do you accuse?"

Challenor gave no direct answer. He turned to Anthony. "I think, Mr Bassey, you yourself heard the voice last night?"

"I did."

"Was it a voice you knew?"

Anthony hesitated. "I – I am not sure. Since you ask, I think I have heard it somewhere before. There was something familiar. But the words were declaimed – the man was putting on this unearthly tone – as an actor does—"

"Yet you caught something in it that you recognised? Could it have been Huntley's – disguised?"

"Mr Challenor!" cried his lordship sternly.

"I–I cannot say," said Anthony unhappily. "It was all so quick. At the time, I never thought... I suppose it is not impossible... But I can't say. I'm not certain of anything now."

"This is a terrible suggestion," said Ravenwood. "How can you possibly justify it?"

"Where *was* Huntley, my lord, when the rest of us were searching the house? And isn't it strange – the first night the ghost was seen and vanished into the gallery – that Mr Bassey rushed in and immediately encountered Huntley? And who else is a master of creating strange effects and apparitions? Indeed, boasts of his past experience!"

"But only for an entertainment!" Ravenwood appealed to Anthony. "Can *you* see any reason to suspect Huntley?"

Anthony was growing more bewildered than ever. "There is one thing that puzzles me."

"What?"

"He is strangely emphatic that he has never been in this house before – or even in Herefordshire. He has stressed it more than once. Yet I was struck from the very first, he seemed entirely at home in it—"

"Now *you* are fancying things. I had never laid eyes

on him until we met in London."

"I am sorry, my lord. It was merely a feeling I had."

"And why, in Heaven's name, should he of all men want to wreck my plans? His own masque would have to be abandoned!"

"*My* masque," the poet protested in a vicious undertone.

"I can't believe there is anything in your imaginings, either of you," said Ravenwood. "Still – to satisfy you – I will ask Sir Renold what he thinks."

They had only a few hours to wait. Mandeville and Tobias were back by six o'clock. In his room, washing and changing after a warm day in the saddle, Mandeville seemed in high good humour. His mother was always at her best, he remarked, when he could get her off present business and draw out her memories of the past.

"Did you learn anything useful?" Anthony ventured to ask.

"I hope so." Mandeville chuckled from the depths of the shirt he was pulling over his head. "I went in quest of one thing – and found another. I thought my mother, who knows all the oddities of this country, might know of a white witch—"

"A witch?"

"Some harmless old hag that the people in these parts believe in – someone who would come here, cast a few spells, and convince the men that this supposed curse had been lifted. Then at least the work would continue until the next manifestation." Mandeville changed tack abruptly, as though to avoid revealing more about his visit to Wildhope. "How did your day go?"

Anthony recounted, with some satisfaction, his researches in the muniment room. "That was shrewd of you," said Mandeville approvingly. "But you have missed one point which finally proves that our ghost is an impostor."

"What's that, sir?" Anthony was defensive, feeling

slightly nettled.

"I'm more at fault than you. I must have known, years ago, that Crucorney was a Cistercian house, but I had clean forgotten until you mentioned the word just now. When we were in Italy, we saw Cistercian monks." Mandeville smiled quizzically.

"I–I don't understand—"

"White habits, Anthony! But few people in England have ever seen a monk – they picture them all in dark colours. So our ill-informed phantom chose the wrong disguise."

Anthony laughed, sharing his pleasure in the discovery. Lady Ravenwood should now be completely convinced that it was no supernatural phenomenon troubling her household. But this kind of quibbling argument would scarcely bring back the workmen. And there remained a flesh-and-blood adversary to reckon with.

They went downstairs to find the others. Both Huntley and Challenor were with Ravenwood, disputing some fresh difference over the masque. Anthony wondered if his lordship would take Mandeville aside to tell him of their suspicions about the designer. But it was Mandeville who took the initiative.

"Too fine an evening to be indoors, gentlemen. Shall we walk in the garden?"

"By all means," said Ravenwood. He looked glad of the excuse to escape from the wrangling of the two collaborators.

"In that case," said Huntley crossly, rolling up his sketches, "I'll continue with these alterations."

"No, by your leave, Mr Huntley—" Mandeville's tone was satin smooth, but his hand was on the designer's sleeve. "I would particularly ask you to join us."

"As you please."

They went out with his lordship. Anthony caught a

gleam of pleasant anticipation in Challenor's eye, before the two of them fell in behind the others. "Aha," the poet murmured.

The Priory garden was small, running down towards the river burbling noisily behind the boundary wall. The air was heady with the fragrances of an early summer evening. Mandeville steered the party towards an alcove with benches. As they sat down he remarked, "This will do well. No one will hear what we say. On an evening like this Herefordshire comes near to Paradise. But I believe, neither of you two gentlemen was ever in these parts before?"

"Never," said Huntley. "As I have told you."

"Then now, perhaps, you will tell me – and his lordship – why you keep up this falsehood. And what you were doing when you came to this house before. When you worked for Nicholas Owen!"

Twelve *An Old Secret*

"Nicholas Owen?" echoed the designer huskily.

His aggressive manner changed. "God rest his soul!" he muttered. Instinctively he crossed himself. It was the first indication that he was, or had once been, a Catholic.

"Well?" Mandeville was relentless.

"That's going back thirty years, Sir Renold—"

"No matter."

"I swore a solemn vow—"

"To whom? Owen died in the Tower—"

"Ay, tortured to death, they say."

"Some rough things were done. It was a desperate time – just after the Gunpowder Plot. But Owen is dead. And if your oath was to the Lord Ravenwood of those days, he is dead too. My lord here can release you from it."

"If you'll tell me what this is all about," interrupted Ravenwood. "I'm mystified."

"It was in your uncle's time," Mandeville explained. "He sheltered priests here, so that he and his Catholic neighbours could hear Mass in secret."

"So I've heard. But the sheriff never took him to court – they found no evidence against him."

"Thanks to Owen – and our friend Mr Huntley here."

"How did you discover this?" demanded Huntley.

"My mother cried out at the mention of your name. She has a remarkable memory. She remembers you as a youth, travelling the country with a little man named

Owen – a wonderful craftsman who could turn his hand to any task, carpentry, masonry, bricklaying—"

"That is true. He taught me everything!"

"He was in great demand. Particularly in the big Catholic houses. People realised why, afterwards – after he was caught in Worcestershire, hiding behind one of his own secret panels. Owen devised priest-holes all over this part of the country."

"And never two alike," said Huntley with defiant pride. "If the searchers uncovered one, it never helped them to find another."

"And that's why you're going to help us now." Mandeville looked stern. "We can forgive you for pretending you had not been here before. But you can forget your old promise. Times have changed. Our queen herself is Catholic. My lord is not – and in any case the hiding-places here are no longer needed. My lord does not even know where they are, but over the years the secret has somehow come into the hands of his enemies. I think your duty is plain."

"It is. I see it." Huntley stood up. "Your pardon, my lord. We made five hiding-places. I think I can still find them all."

They were moving off towards the house when Mandeville checked them. "Wait. We know now how our ghost can appear and disappear. But is there a way to get in and out of the house unseen?"

"I never heard of one, Sir Renold. If so, it was a secret he did not share with me. The hiding-places were for the priest if the house were to be suddenly raided by the sheriff. Otherwise, the priest could come and go like anyone else – the servants were loyal, even though they were not all Catholics."

"Then we must go softly. Our ghost may be in one of these places even now. Get Tobias, Anthony. With his lantern. And my pistols. And as Mr Huntley takes us round the house there must be no talking." He turned to

Challenor. "Will you join us?"

"Of course!" But Anthony, as he departed on his errand, thought the poet looked far from happy.

A few minutes later he returned with Tobias to find the four men waiting in the porch. Ravenwood seemed content to let Mandeville take charge. His lordship had had no experience of such affairs.

First they filed after Huntley into the long gallery. He turned, finger on lips, into the second of the bays, where a small writing-table stood and a globe. Then, motioning them to back away in a little semicircle, he stepped silently to the wall and laid his hand on the wainscotting, questing for some remembered spot. The others held their breath. Mandeville had his pistols cocked. The rest had drawn their swords.

There was a faint click. A three-foot panel swung back. They all stared at the oblong of darkness it revealed. For a few moments no one stirred. Then, at a nod from Mandeville, Tobias crept along the wall and, careful to expose only his forearm, shone his lantern inside. The cavity was no more than four feet deep. Anyone hidden there would have been instantly revealed.

It was unlikely that the unknown intruder, if trapped inside the house for any long period, would have chosen such cramped quarters.

The search continued with, at each stopping place, the same precautions.

In the parlour Huntley showed them how a stone slab in front of the fireplace lifted to allow descent into a small chamber measuring about seven feet by six, with a tiny hole that admitted fresh air and a gleam of daylight. Mandeville dropped softly down, then reached up for the lantern. At length he climbed out again, dangling a dusty fragment of bread in fastidious fingers.

They all exchanged meaningful glances, but remembered his injunction not to talk. That bread, thought

Anthony, was not baked many days ago. A mouse would not have left it uneaten. A man had been in the chamber recently.

In his lordship's study Huntley knelt, fingering the wide floorboards, and pulled up a long nail that was loose. His manner here was less cautious, and when, gripping the nail, he lifted the board and those attached on either side, Anthony could understand why. This hiding-place was so shallow that anyone hiding there would have had to lie flat and helpless. Huntley explained afterwards that this had been made as a storage place for the priest's vestments and altar furnishings.

Anthony's heart was pounding uncontrollably as he followed Ravenwood upstairs. Challenor brought up the rear. Despite his airs and graces, he seemed not to mind for once that a young secretary should precede him.

The tension was mounting. Huntley had only two more places to show them. If the supposed monk was still in the house, the chances were that he would be in one of them. And, though he might have escaped immediate discovery last night by mingling with the household, it was hard to believe that he had got clear, clambering over the walls unnoticed in moonlight as bright as day.

On the top floor Huntley took them into a bedchamber, a mean small room not in use. A tall cupboard was built into the wall. He opened it gently, smiling at the disappointment on their faces when they saw it was a mere twelve inches deep, and empty. Then he thrust his head inside and stood for some moments, intently listening. He emerged again, gave Mandeville his usual nod of warning, and stretched his arm into the top of the cupboard. There was a soft whir of well-oiled mechanism, and, as he turned his wrist, the back of the cupboard slid inch by inch to the left.

There was space for them to squeeze through into the

room beyond. The lantern showed where, thirty years before, the youthful Huntley and his master had bricked up a window and a door. The light shone too on drips of recent candle-grease and an empty bottle that still smelt of wine.

They climbed out again. Challenor awaited them, fidgeting nervously with his sword. He alone had been unwilling to soil his lace in the investigation.

They made their way past several attics and reached the head of the backstairs. The designer led them down one flight, and paused, pointing into a small room still rosily lit by the sunset. They crowded in behind him, momentarily dazzled by the brilliance flooding in through the bow window. There was a broad window-seat, with shabby cushions, split and stained. A broken toy suggested that Margaret and Gilbert might at one time have used the place for their play, and then childlike tired of it.

Huntley reached out to the cushions, as if to push them aside.

The corners rose in his fingers, responding to his pull, but neither cushion came away. Mandeville stepped forward and peered. So far as Anthony could see from behind, each cushion was stuck, at some roughly central point, to the wooden seat on which it lay. It could have been accidental. More candle-grease, or a child's squashed sweetmeat. But when, at a sign from Mandeville, Huntley pressed some hidden latch, the whole bench slanted upwards and the cushions merely drooped, without sliding off, ready to flop back into position when the seat was lowered again.

But the seat was not lowered.

Mandeville stooped, took a quick peep through the aperture, and jerked his head back in the nick of time as a pistol snapped from below, a bullet thudded into the plaster ceiling overhead, and acrid smoke gushed up into the room.

"Tobias! The lantern!"

Mandeville snatched it, and, without exposing himself, tried to direct its light down into the gloom.

He was repaid with a second shot. Before the smoke thinned he pointed his own weapon downwards and discharged it. Then, setting down the lantern, and keeping only his other pistol, he thrust his leg over the side of the window-seat.

"Take care!" cried Ravenwood.

And Huntley flung out a powerful arm to restrain him. "We have him trapped, sir! There's no need—"

"He's running!" said Mandeville curtly, and dropped from their sight.

Anthony's slimness gave him an advantage. Eel-like, he slipped between his elders, caught a fleeting glimpse of a twilit floor ten feet below him, and let himself go.

He landed lightly, spun round, and almost tripped over a ladder laid across the boards. In the grey gloom, with the fumes still eddying and reeking in his nostrils, he could see neither Mandeville nor the intruder. Then, as he blinked round in perplexity, he was aware of a blacker patch in the far corner of the room, and coming from it the fading clatter of descending footsteps.

He made for it. A nail-studded door met his outspread hand. It was open, pushed back against the wall. His feet found a step, and then another, spiralling downwards. As he shuffled, testing for safe foothold, there was a massive thud behind him and the lantern-light danced, throwing his shadow wavering in front. "Mind, lad!" cried Tobias in his ear, and shoved him aside.

There was at least more light now, though it washed madly to and fro on the curving masonry as Tobias rushed helter-skelter down the twisting stairs.

Anthony followed, risking his neck so as not to lose the lantern's guidance. There were voices below, echoing eerily in the confined space. Mandeville's . . . and another's. The voice he had heard from the roof last night. The voice he had heard – he now recognised it in a flash of enlightenment – on that first morning when they were surprised by Ruthin and his gang at the castle.

He caught another sound, the rush of water. Tobias splashed into it first, and gasped. Anthony was only moments after him. At the bottom stair the water swirled round his ankles, ice cold but at least only a few inches deep. The bobbing lantern gleamed on it. They were in a tunnel, stonework arching just over their heads, the water streaming away in front. They plunged on, staggering, slithering, clutching at the dank walls for support.

Now there was pale daylight ahead, a curving whiteness broken by the dancing silhouettes of Mandeville and his quarry. Over Tobias's shoulder Anthony saw them interlock in a grotesque embrace of manikins.

"Hold him, sir!" bellowed Tobias.

But, after another moment of frenzied struggling, one figure detached itself and sped on, and the other, suddenly shapeless, seemed to crumple and fall. When Tobias and Anthony reached the spot, Mandeville was scrambling to his feet again, dripping and cursing volubly. "Hold this," he said savagely, thrust a great weight of sodden cloth into Anthony's hand, and raced on towards the outlet.

The three of them burst into the daylight almost together. There was a jumble of rocks and bushes. They were close under the first arch of Crucorney Bridge, and the river was rushing past their feet. Of the fugitive there was no sign.

Tobias flung out his arm and pointed downstream. "There he goes!"

Already thirty yards away a curious object, like an immense wicker basket, was spinning away on the rapid current. A man crouched in it, plying a paddle. As they stood, helpless, the river swept him out of sight behind its piled boulders and clustering willows.

"The oldest trick," said Mandeville sourly. "I thought I had him. And he slipped out of his robe."

Anthony looked down at the soggy bundle he was holding, and held it at arm's length. It was a monk's habit, dark with wet, but grey.

Thirteen *Her Majesty's Pleasure*

Ravenwood and Huntley stumbled panting from the bushes screening the mouth of the tunnel.

"I never knew of the passage," cried Huntley in an aggrieved tone. "They must have thought me too young to trust with that secret—"

Ravenwood was not interested in his excuses. "Where has he gone?" he demanded impatiently of Mandeville.

"Down river. He had a coracle hidden—"

"We'll ride after him!"

"Waste of time. He can land anywhere and vanish. By the time we have the horses saddled—" Mandeville shrugged his shoulders disgustedly. "Also, it will soon be dark. Still, we know who it was. Ruthin. He gave himself away when he shouted."

"He won't get into the house again," said Ravenwood grimly. He turned and led them scrambling through the wilderness under the bridge to reach the road. There seemed no purpose in splashing their way back through the tunnel, and they gained a certain satisfaction from the astonished faces of Challenor and her ladyship when they reappeared in the house, wet and dishevelled, from outside.

At least everything was now quite plain. Somehow Ruthin had learnt the old secret of the Priory. Several people must once have shared it with the Catholic lord, and, in the years between, one of them must have talked.

"But the tunnel!" said Anthony. "If you knew nothing of it, Mr Huntley, Nicholas Owen could never have built it by himself!"

"Nay, not in a lifetime. That tunnel dates back long before his day."

"It must be an old monastery drain," Ravenwood explained. "The monks liked running water. There are streams everywhere in this valley. They must have diverted one through the precincts. It was lost sight of in all the rebuilding."

The coracle had enabled Ruthin to reach the mouth of the tunnel unobserved. The lightweight fisherman's craft would glide silently over the shallowest parts of the river, and could be easily lifted over obstructions and concealed.

There was a liveliness at supper that night such as Anthony had not seen since the evening of his first visit.

Lady Ravenwood sparkled, her fears of a real ghost finally removed. Challenor had recovered his confidence and was almost witty. Even Huntley mellowed, and entertained them with his boyhood recollections of that earlier lord who had commissioned the priest-holes. And the servants, coming and going around the table, were all smiles.

The door to the secret staircase was safely barricaded overnight. Next morning, Huntley insisted that bricks and mortar be carried into the house and that he, and he alone, should wall up the doorway. "A good notion, Will," said Mandeville approvingly. "Why waste a good secret? One day you might be glad of it." And Ravenwood laughed, unable to imagine such a situation.

Meanwhile, on his orders, the bare story of the previous evening was put round the estate. The monk's habit was nailed, spread-eagled, on the outer gate of the Priory for all to see, as dead vermin might be displayed by a gamekeeper. Still not a word was said about the impostor's identity. If Ruthin did not realise that it was known, he might be less wary in any further attempt he planned.

At least the story of the curse was scotched for ever. By noon the workmen were streaming back to the castle, eager to make up for lost time and their previous timidity.

With things going so smoothly, Huntley was able to leave for London. Now that he knew exactly what he required for the masque, there was much to be arranged. He would be back in a month or two, he promised, with a whole convoy of waggons. Ravenwood, taking no chances, would supply an armed escort to ensure they were not molested on the road.

Challenor also returned to town, but after waiting a day or two, to avoid travelling with the designer. He was clearly home-sick for the amusements of London, and, with the anxieties of the ambitious, knew it was unwise to drop out of the social scene for too long. But he would be back in good time, he announced, to make sure when rehearsals started that his inspired verses were not further cut about by uncultured mechanics.

It was from Challenor, therefore, hovering on the outer fringe of the fashionable world at Whitehall, that Amoret first heard the latest news from Crucorney.

She was vastly relieved. If she managed to prevail upon their Majesties to lodge two or three nights at the Priory, she did not want the royal repose shattered by midnight apparitions.

That fear removed, she felt fairly satisfied with the way things were going.

The Queen seemed pleased to see her back at court. It was understandable. Most of the other ladies round her had been chosen for their high standing and respectability. They were rather dull, thought Amoret, and some of them on the old side. And the King, though obviously a devoted and adoring husband, was a stiff and solemn little man, who raised a shocked eyebrow if Henrietta Maria gave way, for a moment, to the kittenish gaiety which was a part of her nature. I suppose, Amoret told herself, I make a change. Any young girl would. After all, though the Queen had borne several children, she was still only in her mid-twenties. She remained, in tastes and instincts, very much the impulsive, emotional young Frenchwoman in this unsympathetic alien land.

If the Queen had a warm welcome for her Maid of Honour, someone else had not.

Lockerbie could barely hide his vexation when he first encountered Amoret. "A delightful surprise," he said. "I thought you had left the service of Her Majesty?"

"Oh, no, my lord." She stood her ground, outfacing him. It took all her nerve. The Marquis was a formidable adversary. "I had leave to go into the country."

"You would have been wise to stay there. The country is healthier."

"I know. But soon the whole court will be going there. So your lordship need not fear for my well-being."

He passed on. He would never forgive her, she knew, for rejecting his advances.

But the veiled dislike in his eyes that day was nothing compared with his expression when they met a few days later at a ball.

"They tell me you have been at Crucorney?"

He was, she could see, eaten up with curiosity. Eager for her version of what had been happening there. Unaware, though, that she – or even Ravenwood himself – knew anything of his own involvement.

"Yes," she said lightly. "My brother and I were travelling through that country. He wished to see Lord Ravenwood's horses. His lordship made us most welcome. He is a fine gentleman."

"Oh, very fine! And means to be finer – with these

vast building projects. I gather you have been extolling them to the Queen—"

"She questioned me."

"And you answered – eloquently. She has a notion to see them for herself, if she can work upon His Majesty. And this great entertainment Lord Ravenwood is planning."

"It will be wonderful. She would enjoy it mightily."

"A pity it is quite impossible."

"Impossible, my lord?"

The music was cover to their talk. They could fence frankly, no one overhearing.

"The King never travels so far west on his summer progress. And so many vie for the honour of entertaining him. The tour tends to follow a pattern – it is customary, and easier, to stay at the same houses that have lodged the court in earlier years—"

"Would it not be better if His Majesty saw fresh faces?"

"Perhaps. But to miss some noble family which has entertained him before – it would be taken as a slight—"

"Or a rebuke?" she suggested wickedly. "There is one house – in Berkshire, I think it is – where the noble lord has displeased the King with some scandal or other. His Majesty is strict. I need not tell your lordship that." She met his cold eyes boldly. "He might omit that visit. With a little shuffling of the timetable he could then fit in Crucorney."

"No doubt you will suggest it!"

"*I*, my lord?" She opened her own eyes wide in innocence. "*I* can do nothing. You will excuse me now? They are going to play a coranto." She dropped him a contemptuous curtsey, and darted off to take her place in the dance.

Ten days later, at the Priory, Ravenwood broke the seal of the letter he had been hoping for. It was brief, almost curt, like the King's spoken words, but it was in his own hand:

Ravenwood,

    This is to tell you that Her Majesty and I are minded to see the new castle you are building and the masque that we hear is to be played there this summer. Our progress already brings us into Gloucestershire, and a little alteration will permit us to pass some few days with you. As to when, and how long, how many persons, the number of servants and horses to be provided for, you will be informed.

Charles R.

Ravenwood read it aloud to his wife and guests. He was triumphant. "Isn't this wonderful? My cup is full!"

"Your house will be," said Mandeville dryly.

And as Anthony studied all their faces his heart went out to Lady Ravenwood, torn between pleasure in her husband's happiness and horror at the domestic responsibilities that lay ahead.

The same post had brought her a letter from Amoret. While the others were intently discussing the great news in all its aspects, her ladyship drew Anthony aside with an understanding smile. "This was enclosed for you. Doubtless some message from her brother."

"Doubtless, madam," he answered gravely.

He bowed, and slipped away to open it alone.

Somewhat like the King, Amoret wrote as she talked, but the effect was very different. Her pen had fairly jigged across the paper.

    . . . So, it is decided. We are coming. My lord L. is near mad with fury. He, that is commonly most like one of those glaciers in Savoy, now resembles more a volcano smouldering. He has thought of a dozen reasons why we should not travel to Crucorney, but H.M. has an answer to them all — or does not trouble with an answer, only says it is her pleasure. She can be most obstinate. Fortunately I have learned to play on her fancies, like our small friend on his

violin, and now she will have it so, and of course her loving husband will deny her nothing.

It was most fortunate, wrote Amoret, and in one way surprising. In most matters the Queen was sympathetic to Lockerbie's views. Like him, she wanted the King to take a strong line with his subjects. She had no use for weakness. Argumentative gentlemen, who talked of ancient English liberties, should be clapped into the Tower and left to think again. Seditious pamphlets, criticising the King's government, should be seized and burnt. Their authors and printers should stand in the pillory. But on this question of the masque she differed from the Marquis and would have her way. He too, after all, was but a subject, even though he had been fast rising, in recent months, to a position of dominance.

Fortunate too, thought Anthony, that Her Majesty had no inkling of Ravenwood's moderate views and concern for the common people. If this Crucorney visit had the desired effect, and Ravenwood won office at court, with a place in the King's Council, she might be less pleased with the influence he brought to bear.

Meanwhile, Amoret turned from these tedious political questions to those which were of more immediate interest. She went on:

H.M. is sorry that she herself can take no part in the masque, but her doctors say that the progress will bring sufficient fatigue, so advise against it. We others have permission. So bid Mr H. to provide us with several dances, corantoes and galliards and some lively country dance, perhaps the Soldiers March or Huff Hamukin, and fine costumes for all, but nothing difficult, for we shall have at most two days to learn our parts in the entertainment. Be sure not to forget the saraband he spoke of, with us all dressed as shadows in robes of black taffeta with black vizards and coronets of stars. Provided he contrives for the lights to come bright on a sudden, simulating the sunrise as Pegasus

150

descends, so that we can throw off our robes of darkness and be seen in cloth-of-gold and aurora colour, more splendid than anything we have worn in the scenes before . . .

Anthony made a face as he read. He could not see himself standing over Huntley and conveying all these instructions. The courtiers would have to wear what the designer had prepared for them.

The letter ended,

For discretion, write to Z in his own language. Any message enclosed will be welcomed by your constant and faithful friend, A.

He wrote back the next day, telling her the latest news. The Little Castle was now furnished. The Raven-woods were moving there at once, and he with them, for Mandeville seemed likely to remain with his friend till this whole business was safely concluded. The Priory itself was now to be refurbished and made ready to receive the royal party. As for Mr H., he was expected any day now from London, with everything necessary for the performance.

Sure enough, on the following afternoon, there came a servant riding ahead to announce that Huntley would arrive by nightfall, and the sun was still above the westward hills when the waggons began to trundle into the Priory courtyard.

"It looks like a siege-train," said Mandeville as they welcomed the designer. "As though you had come to assault my lord's new castle, not perform there."

Huntley grinned as he slid stiffly from the saddle. "When his lordship has seen the bills he is more like to say it is a treasure-train. But I have guarded it well, all these many miles."

"It shall be guarded here, too. Things have been quiet since you left us. But it would be folly to assume the game is won."

Some of the waggons were backed into empty barns, others were marshalled, wheel to wheel, in the open courtyard. It was all practice for the outdoor servants, who in a few weeks would be called upon to solve more difficult puzzles when the royal party arrived. Tomorrow Huntley would say what he needed first up at the castle, and what could stay here until it was required.

"I think," Mandeville murmured to Ravenwood, "I will sleep down here, in my old room, with Anthony and Tobias. As our friend said, we have a treasure-train stowed here."

Ravenwood thanked him, and looked slightly relieved. Though there had been no further sign from Sir Dudley Ruthin, though the secret entrance had been safely walled up and the patrols of watchmen and dogs maintained, he would sleep sounder tonight, he admitted, if Renold were in charge.

They all supped together in the handsome pillar chamber of the Little Castle, the sunset glowing on the carved alabaster and the chequered marble floor, until the candles were needed and drew all eyes to the mural paintings above the wainscotting. Even Huntley had tact enough to admire the work of other artists, though he could not long keep off the subject of his purchases in London and the effects they would produce upon the stage.

Mandeville seemed restive. At last, with an apologetic look at Lady Ravenwood, he made a move to break up the party, Mr Huntley must be tired after his week on the road, he would be glad of some sleep. Lady Ravenwood, who was always tired these days without needing to budge from Crucorney, smiled gratefully and made only the feeblest effort to detain them. Good-nights were said, and leaving the Ravenwoods in their fine new quarters the other three strolled down through the warm dusk to the Priory.

Huntley was indeed ready for his bed. Mandeville showed not the least eagerness for sleep. "I think I'll watch awhile," he told Anthony. "If need be, I'll wake Tobias and he can relieve me. No—" He declined Anthony's dutiful offer. "But *he* can call you if he wants you to take over for a spell."

"Thank you, sir. Then – good-night."

"Good-night."

Mandeville's footsteps faded downstairs. Thus relieved of responsibility, Anthony laid his head on the pillow and was almost immediately asleep.

It was towards the end of the short summer night that Tobias roused him. Tobias was, in fact, rousing the entire house. He burst into Anthony's room like a bellowing bull, and then rushed through to wake his master.

"W-what's the matter?" Anthony mumbled, blinking into wakefulness. And then, through the window, he saw the answer for himself.

The western sky was aglow. Under it, the long façade of the castle ran along the ridge. The Banqueting House and the Gallery were like a giant fire-grate, belching sparks and flame.

Fourteen *"Pegasus Will Fly—"*

Mandeville sprang fully dressed from his bed, needing only to draw on his boots and buckle on his sword. "We won't wait for horses. As quick on foot." He rushed downstairs. Anthony followed as fast as he could, and overtook him while the porter was still fumbling to unbar the gates.

Mandeville turned to Tobias. "You stay here. Be doubly on your guard. This may be a trick to draw us away from here." The gate swung back, he was through, and Anthony after him. As they ran over the bridge they heard the bars crash back into place behind them.

"They need some one like Tobias," panted Mandeville. "He'll not be fooled. We've got all the hands we need up there."

They reached the zigzag track and toiled up the steep face of the hill. Smoke eddied down in their faces, stinging wood-smoke, dimming the angry pink of the sky overhead. Through the roar and crackle of the blaze they could hear voices, orders shouted and answered. There were, as Mandeville had said, plenty of men at the castle. Besides the watchmen on duty, something like half the household servants had moved into their new quarters.

They reached the terrace, brightly lit up by the

flaming roof of the Great Gallery. There was a living chain of men passing buckets from the little stone conduit house, where water came by pipe from a spring. Intrepid figures were running up tall ladders and doing their pitiful best to quench the fire.

Ravenwood was directing operations. He turned to greet them, all grime and sweat, his white shirt blotched.

"It's no good," he gasped. "The timbers were too well alight. No accident, either. There was a charge of gunpowder to start it off – and then a barrel of tar, I'd swear from the smell, and other easy kindling stuff—"

"Where in God's name were the watchmen?" Mandeville demanded.

"I'm not clear. Some rigmarole – a hooded figure—"

"Oh, not *that* again?" Mandeville groaned disgustedly.

His lordship shouted to the men on the ladders to come down. It was a waste of effort, and he would not have them risk their lives. The roof could not be saved. Charred timbers were crashing down at intervals, and there was a perilous stream of molten lead. The only thing was to ensure that the fire did not spread to other buildings. Ravenwood flung himself energetically into this work. Anthony followed his example, and only later realised that his master was no longer with them.

Mandeville reappeared as the dawn was breaking and they were all clustered round, contemplating the damage. The fire had burnt itself out. The Gallery and Banqueting Hall was a smoke-smeared shell, open to the sky. The walls stood, marvellously unharmed, save where the window-frames had gone. But within, the fine plasterwork, the painting and gilding were all to do again.

"It will take months," said a doleful voice. Anthony found Huntley at his side, assessing the destruction with an expert tradesman's eye. He had just come up from the

155

Priory, where everything had remained quiet.

Lady Ravenwood appeared, holding tightly to the children, who were in tears. Anthony had never seen her so angry. "Monsters!" she said chokingly. "This was my lord's *dream*. And in a few short minutes—!" She almost broke down.

Mandeville came along the terrace in earnest conversation with Ravenwood. The others gathered round, eager for news.

The watchmen had indeed seen a hooded figure. But, to do them justice, they had not acted from fear. Knowing it was no ghost, they had gone in chase of it, hoping to catch the impostor and drag him triumphantly before his lordship. Which, said Mandeville, had been precisely what it was hoped they would do. The ghost always showed itself with the deliberate intention of being seen – in this case so that the watchmen should be lured away to the far side of the castle, giving other intruders a chance to start the fire.

The plan had worked splendidly. Ruthin – or whoever had played the spectre – had made good his escape. And so had the party – there must have been several men to do the work so swiftly – who had kindled the blaze. All would have been well away, under cover of the night, while the watchmen were raising the alarm and making their first frenzied efforts to extinguish the flames.

Ravenwood was comforting his wife. "There's nothing that cannot be put right—"

"But not in the time, Will! Look at it. The roof alone. And all that beautiful work. Not if the craftsmen worked twenty-four hours in every day. It can never be ready for the King." Margaret and Gilbert set up a wail of disappointment. Their mother turned to Huntley. "This is a sad blow to you, too. Your wonderful masque – to have all your labours utterly wasted—"

"Wait." Mandeville broke in. He turned to his friend. "If I know you, you won't let even this beat you."

"I will not! Though what I can do, for the life of me, I—"

"The Riding House! Mr Huntley, could you stage the masque in the Riding House?"

The designer's eyes lit up. "Why not? Give me a few minutes – a measurement or two—" And he was off, heedless of the drifting smoke and the general scene of ruin and despair.

Ravenwood gave some more instructions to his men and then, with Mandeville and Anthony, trudged wearily off to the Little Castle. Standing somewhat apart as it did, it had suffered no more than drifting clouds of pungent smoke. Their hostess had gone before them. Basins of warm water and towels were quickly ready, food and drink set out.

"Dear God, I can't endure much more of this," said Lady Ravenwood.

"Nor shall you, Rose. But I won't be beaten by a half-crazy ruffian, who bears a grudge for some old dispute between our grandfathers."

"It is rather more than that," Mandeville reminded him gently. "It is Lockerbie you are fighting. Ruthin is just a convenient tool he has found in this neighbourhood – the perfect agent for this purpose."

"But – this Lockerbie! I can still scarcely credit it," she said. "There have always been rivals for court favour. Under every king, under Elizabeth. There have been plots and intrigues and scandals. But, Renold – this devilish campaign—"

"Lockerbie is an unusual man. He's fighting for his future. There isn't room at the King's side for him and Will together. Will's too honest." Mandeville's saturnine features softened as he glanced at his friend. "If Will is at court he will speak his mind. Things will be uncovered. It will be the end of Lockerbie."

"It seems more likely to be the end of us," she said gloomily.

"No, sweetheart," said Ravenwood. "From now on, things shall be different." He turned to Mandeville. "We've been too easy. Like some peace-loving fellow boxing unwillingly with a scoundrel – waiting to be hit. And, if we've parried a blow, thinking he won't hit us again."

"Certainly, our precautions haven't been enough."

"We'll change all that. Until this royal visit is over, both Castle and Priory must be guarded as closely as though we were at war."

"We *are* at war."

"True. And we can't fight with a few watchmen and dogs. We need men trained to use weapons." Ravenwood made a quick calculation. "On this estate alone I have two dozen men who are enrolled in the train bands – sound men, small tenants mostly. I can't call them out *as* militia, only the Lord Lieutenant can do that, but I can ask their help as individuals. I can get another score from my other estates further away—"

"And I'll find you half a dozen from Wildhope. Though Heaven knows what my mother will say," Mandeville added with a smile, "taking farmers from their work at the busiest season."

"I would not wish to vex your mother—"

Who would, thought Anthony?

"No matter, Neighbours must help each other."

"No one shall lose by it," his lordship promised earnestly. "I have an even greater favour to ask of you yourself."

"Yours to command, Will."

"No – the commanding is to be done by you. I shall have a few other matters on my mind for the next month or two. Will *you* take charge of these defences – act, as it were, as commander of our garrison?"

"Most willingly!"

"Oh, thank you, Renold!" exclaimed Lady Ravenwood. "That will truly be a burden off my mind."

Huntley rejoined them just then, eyes alight at the prospect of fresh problems to solve. He helped himself without ceremony to a tankard of small beer, and folded a cold sausage inside a slice of buttered bread.

"Everything will be all right," he announced contentedly.

"We are relieved to hear it," said Mandeville ironically.

"The dimensions are not so different. My scenery will adapt easily to the Riding House. The walls can be hung with tapestry – a boarded floor must be laid, of course—"

"And there is already the spectators' gallery, where their Majesties can sit," suggested Ravenwood.

Huntley stared. "They certainly cannot," he said bluntly. He licked his fingers, took a noisy swig of beer, and stretched out for another piece of bread. "They will sit downstairs – on a raised platform with thrones, by all means—"

"But, Mr Huntley – surely—"

"I need that balcony for my machines. Fortunately, it is most solidly built. It will take the weight of my contrivances." His belligerent expression quelled any objection. "You wish Pegasus to fly through the air, don't you? And Perseus? You want clouds to drift across the stage? You want mountains to yawn open? Grecian temples to appear and disappear? A dark stage to blaze suddenly with the light of a thousand lamps and candles? For such things I must have a loft high above the stage, with cables and winches and pulleys – and men to work them. So, I must have the balcony. The audience must sit facing it. Or rather the stage I shall construct beneath it. The balcony itself will be hidden. There will be a proscenium arch to hide it – and a great painted curtain to hang from it until the masque begins."

He was unanswerable. Ravenwood could only say,

159

feebly, "You must do everything, Mr Huntley, as you think best."

"I shall, my lord. Or you waste your money in employing me."

Lady Ravenwood ventured to point out that, though all might be plain sailing now for the performance, the illustrious company would have to eat beforehand. The Great Gallery could no more be restored in time for the banquet than the hall made fit for the masque. Delightful as it might be to use the terrace or the gardens, there was always the chance of a wet day. Indeed, she hinted, my lord's enemies were quite capable of arranging even that.

Huntley, however, brushed aside her fears. "Canvas pavilions, madam. Or canvas stretched like a ceiling over the gallery itself. With enough rich hangings – with candle-light to distract the eye from detail – it can be very fine. Have no fear. I will sketch out the manner of it for my lord. When time allows. But first the masque!"

It was a day of furious activity, everyone working with a will to clear up the debris of the fire. Mandeville made his own dispositions. By midday he had mustered the nucleus of his defence force. The remainder would take a day or two to gather. Most of them had pikes or muskets, but those with good sporting guns were asked to bring them – a fowling piece could be better relied upon to hit some fleeting figure in the dark.

Mandeville divided his men, since both houses must be protected. He wanted Tobias with him at the Castle. In any case, he could not expect the household at the Priory to take orders from his man-servant. So an experienced old militia officer, Captain Lawson, was put in charge there, with the sole task of keeping the old mansion safe for the King's lodging. Huntley's waggons, with their priceless contents, were driven up to the Castle and stowed safe under cover before night-fall. Thus Mandeville had all the most essential things concentrated under his own eye.

For Anthony he had a special duty.

"I am lending you to Mr Huntley," he said with a smile.

"To Mr Huntley?" Anthony stared. "What am I to do?"

"Run round very busily, with a notebook and pencil in your hand, and an important expression on your face. Sometimes you may sit down – wherever it seems good to you – and scribble or calculate, it does not matter what, so long as no one casts eyes on your jottings." Mandeville burst out laughing. "Have no fear. Mr Huntley knows. And approves – so far as he ever approves of anything. You may do what the devil you like, he says, provided you don't get under his feet or hinder his men."

"I see. I am observing?"

"Just that. From now onwards this place will be full of fresh faces. It can't be otherwise. All these strangers fetched down from London – without them, it's impossible to present the masque. True, Huntley vouches for them. He has worked with most of them before. They are all, of course, highly skilled in their various crafts."

"It would be hard for the Marquis to plant his own men among them."

"But not so hard, perhaps, to buy one of the craftsmen themselves. They're not overpaid. Certainly they are not paid in a month what Lockerbie would offer for one night's work. Someone might be tempted."

"I'll keep my eyes open – and my ears," said Anthony doubtfully.

"You can do no more. Huntley, of course, will be everywhere, supervising every detail – so far as the work is concerned, nothing will escape *his* eye. But if there were some ill-intentioned fellow, planning further trouble, he would be on his guard against Huntley."

"Whereas who would suspect a simple-looking

young fellow like me?"

"You have the notion exactly." Mandeville clapped him on the shoulder.

At night Huntley would have a bed made up in the gallery of the Riding House, with armed guards inside and out. But Anthony would sleep in the Little Castle, for otherwise his real function would become obvious to all.

Meanwhile, in Whitehall, the Maids of Honour prepared for the court's customary summer progress across a chosen part of the kingdom.

The mid-June heat had struck London. The town stank. There was the usual anxiety lest plague break out. The playhouses closed. The sun might be bright, but everything else was dull. The roads were firm and dry, if dusty. The countryside beckoned.

The older ladies recalled the great houses they would be revisiting. Acid comments were mingled with sentimental memories. Amoret listened and, as the only person who had ever seen Crucorney, was herself consulted as a source of information.

Then came a shock, followed by a day and night of intolerable suspense. Strolling in the drought-parched garden she encountered Lockerbie. Instead of coldly passing by, he paused and greeted her with almost a smirk.

"I fear you will be deprived of your return visit to Crucorney."

She kept calm with an effort. "What do you mean, my lord?"

"It is said there has been a great fire there, and the new castle burnt to the ground. A sad calamity. The Lord Chamberlain awaits formal word from Ravenwood, but already he is considering how to change the plans for that stage of the journey." He bowed and walked on.

It was not until after dinner the next day that Zorzi, under pretence of showing her his music, slipped her a letter in Anthony's handwriting. It ran:

We had some trouble last night, and I write at once to assure you – whatever may come to be rumoured at court, preparations are continuing for their M's entertainment as arranged. The wings of Pegasus may be a little singed, but he will fly nonetheless. I have no time to write more – Ld R. is sending post haste to confirm that all will be in order for the court's coming, so I must seal this packet and send it by the same messenger. Yr devtd and assrd friend, A. B.

From the Queen herself, next day, she learned a little more. There had been a fire at Crucorney and some damage done, but not as serious as feared.

As soon as she was alone, she pulled out Anthony's letter and looked at the date. It had made good time from Herefordshire and Zorzi had been prompt to pass it on. Anthony himself must have been writing within hours of the event.

Yet the Marquis had been a full day earlier with the news. It confirmed her suspicions. She sat down at once to write back to Crucorney.

Fifteen *The Riding House*

Anthony tackled his daunting assignment with a conscientious thoroughness that would have satisfied even Lady Mandeville.

Work in the Riding House started with the erection of a spacious platform on trestles, the gallery overhead being extended and adapted to serve as a stage-loft from which the usual theatrical machines could be operated.

Until the dance floor should be laid down, and the seating installed, the rest of the building was available as a vast open workshop, in which the scene-painters and others could get busy on their various tasks.

Through this hive of activity Anthony moved freely and, he hoped, unobtrusively. The lofty building resounded with voices and hammerings, the rasp of saws, the purr of well-oiled pulleys, the thud and thump and scrape of heavy objects being shifted. The air smelt of wood-shavings and glue, size and paint, rolls of fresh canvas, and the sweat of human effort. All work requiring fire was strictly confined to the great forge adjoining – it stood between the Riding House proper and the first range of stables beyond, part of the same magnificent architectural design, yet safely walled off. In the Riding House, now filling with inflammable materials, Huntley took no chances. Even Ravenwood would not have dared to smoke his pipe there.

Anthony had begun by privately obtaining copies of the pay-rolls naming every workman who had rightful business in the Riding House or in the forge. In the first few days he applied himself to identifying each by name and face. The notebook had a double usefulness, not only as cover for his presence but for the jotting down of helpful details. Lest some other eye should fall on these, he disguised their nature with scraps of Italian, or other languages remembered from school, designating a red-bearded carpenter as *barba rossa* and a chatterbox scene-painter as *paroquet*. He took pains to observe the relations between each man and his particular work-mates, alert for the slightest indication that anyone was a newcomer. He listened not only to what was said between them but to the way in which it was said. The way men looked at each other, the old jokes they shared, the obvious understanding that existed between them, working in harmony with often not a syllable exchanged . . .

He could spy no stranger. At the end of a week he was able, by persistence, to tick the last of the names. Most of these men had worked together, off and on, for years. He could not discover one who was not obviously acquainted with several of the others.

So the Marquis had not managed to plant some complete outsider among these men. It was something to feel sure of that. But there was the other possibility Mandeville had suggested: one of the regular workmen might have been bribed to make some further mischief that could still prevent the royal visit.

How could such a man be detected? Not, Anthony admitted gloomily, just by making schoolmasterly ticks against names on a list. Only by tireless vigilance, and, God willing, a measure of good luck. He must continue to watch and listen. Though, as the days passed, his work was simplified. He was getting to know the men. There were some for whose complete honesty he would have pledged his life. There were others who for a variety of reasons – the very young, the very old, and the obviously very simple – seemed most improbable choices for any villainous scheme. He finally came down to a mere half-dozen men who, though they in no way roused his suspicion, seemed to deserve continued observation. Men who, if they had been bought over by Lockerbie's agents, had the wit to hide their intentions and the boldness for effective action.

He shared his thoughts with Tobias, who as always was a tower of strength. Tobias had his other duties, but at odd times he had an easy way of mingling with the workmen, especially when they were relaxing in the courtyard over their beer and tobacco. Tobias, with his knowledge of London's criminal underworld and of human weakness in general, might see through a veneer of apparent innocence that would have fooled Anthony.

Even the Welshman's practised nose could not sniff treachery in all that motley company.

Of course, Anthony consoled himself, the odds were against there being any. It was only one way, and not the easiest, to strike at Ravenwood. Ruthin certainly would find it hard to work through these Londoners, and if he was still pursuing his vendetta he would surely seek another method. But now that all the defences were up, what more could he do? Or Lockerbie? Probably they had both accepted the situation. The royal visit would have to take place, and Ravenwood make of it all he could. A man of Lockerbie's influence must have other shots in his locker. He could still hope to block Ravenwood's advancement at court and save his own position at some later stage.

As Mandeville gave him no fresh duties Anthony continued in the Riding House. He was able now to relax and, while still alert for anything unusual, to take a keen interest in what was going on.

The stage was finished, with its concealed trap-doors and other technical devices. An ornate proscenium arch spanned the building from wall to wall, providing a frame for the actors and dancers who, with Huntley's ever-changing scenery, would compose a sequence of living pictures for the delight of the spectators. High above, well out of sight, the stage-loft, with its dangling ropes and pulleys and wheels, looked like a fantastic blend of belfry, windmill and ship. Up there, you had to be on your guard lest, in gaping at the equipment, you stepped backwards and fell through a gap in the flooring to break your neck on the stage far below.

To begin with, Anthony had been on the poet's side. Affected though young Challenor was, it seemed hard that his verses should be so unceremoniously treated by an uncultured carpenter like Huntley. Anthony still felt sorry for Challenor, but he had come to recognise which of the two men had the genius. To have this privileged position behind the scenes, to see how Huntley's mysterious effects would be achieved, was fascinating.

Huntley, in his own favourite phrase, "would not be questioned", and with other people he remained secretive about his work. But, well aware that Anthony was only there to protect that work, he had admitted him, at first grudgingly, to something as near friendship as he accorded to anyone. Since Anthony must be allowed everywhere, he might as well understand what he saw. Sometimes it satisfied Huntley's vanity to see him baffled by some trick and then casually explain how simple it was – for Huntley – to bring off.

There was, for instance, the little matter of the goddess Athene appearing to Bellerophon in a dream.

"I suppose," said Anthony glancing upwards, "you will fly her down?"

"Certainly not. Already we are going to have the Nine Muses flying round in a circle – and Pegasus – and Pegasus again at the end, when Bellerophon descends on him from the sky. Do you want people to suppose that I have but one idea?" demanded Huntley with assumed ferocity. "Or that I am devising no more than a puppet-show, with everyone on strings?"

"No. But – the goddess can't just *walk* on."

"No need. At one moment she will not be there. At the next she will be. In mid-stage."

"You mean, she'll come up through one of these traps?"

Huntley shook his red head impatiently. "I want her still, like a statue – not thrown up like a stone from a catapult! That is all very well for dancers and acrobats. No. I tell you. The stage is empty, except for Bellerophon, asleep under a tree. Then – Athene is there, in all her divine glory."

"Ah! The scene behind will part to reveal her?"

"Mid-stage, I said. Not up-stage." Despite the withering contempt in his voice, Huntley was clearly delighted with Anthony's perplexity. "The answer is simple." He pointed to a circular hole in the stage floor.

As the hole was barely one inch in diameter Anthony could not see how it would facilitate the appearance on stage of Athene.

"You *will* see," the designer assured him. "Or rather," he added enigmatically, "when this scene is disclosed, in shadow, with the moonbeams falling over yonder to distract the eye, you will *not* see. Nor will anyone else."

It was really a simple illusion which he had used successfully before. A thin iron rod would be pushed through the hole from under the stage. It would stand up seven feet – Huntley was always precise in his measurements. From a thin crossbar at the top of the rod would hang a strip of material, two feet wide, just broad enough to screen the goddess standing motionless behind it. With dim lighting, filmy stuff would be virtually invisible. It would blend into the painted rocks and trees.

"Then – a sudden burst of unearthly music will still further distract the attention of the company," said

Huntley. "That will be the cue for my man beneath the stage to pull down the rod. It will be swift, almost instantaneous. And silent – it needs only a little grease. The cloth will collapse as the rod is pulled down, and being so thin and flimsy it will lie unnoticed on the boards." He chuckled smugly. "There will be too much else to claim people's attention. The goddess will be standing there, seemingly materialised out of thin air. And in a trice, from dark night, the whole scene will blaze with the glory of divinity. I need not tell you how that will be contrived." He could not resist the temptation to do so, nonetheless.

The painted scenery, stretched on prism-shaped frames, would pivot round to produce a transformation. Hundreds of lighted candles, their holders fastened to beams, would swing into position and cast a flood of golden light upon the glittering helmet of Athene. There would be a blast of trumpets. And, Huntley added as an afterthought, the actor playing the goddess would declaim a lot of Mr Challenor's verses.

"Which at least will give us time," he said, "to prepare our next device."

There was another scene in which, according to the ancient myth, Pegasus struck the rock of Mount Helicon with his hoof and caused the sacred spring, Hippocrene, to gush forth. As water would provide problems, and the horse, however realistically modelled, might not manage a convincing kick, the poet had arranged for the incident to take place off-stage, and be described to the audience by a watching nymph in a speech of twenty-two lines. Huntley snorted and cut it to four. Why tell people when you could show them? It was a challenge to his skill. Correctly wired and jointed, his artificial horse could do anything. As for the fountain that was to gush forth, not a drop of water would be needed. A tightly compressed mass of silvery gauze would spring suddenly from a hidden flap in the scenery, unfold, and be kept in continuous agitation by invisible threads. With cunning lighting it would look exactly like sparkling spray.

"This is a mere trifle," he assured Anthony. "If Mr Challenor had given me more scope there could have been a river – nay, a sea, with waves in motion, and ships sailing. Indeed, ships sinking and being wrecked."

There was such a gleam in his eye as his enthusiasm mounted that Anthony hoped the poor poet would arrive soon from London, while any of his work survived.

Challenor rode down a week later, and for days the walls of Crucorney reverberated with their furious disputes.

"It is impossible! It is not in the legend!"

"No matter. It makes a wonderful scene."

"You think everything wonderful if it allows you to bring in another of your absurd devices." Challenor brandished his manuscript, criss-crossed with cuts and changes. "You have ruined my poem!" he cried hysterically.

"Shall I tell you what you may do with your poem?" Huntley glowered back at him. "I have made my lord's masque. That is what matters."

My lord, most unwillingly, was sometimes drawn in as umpire. He could have done without that extra call upon his time. As the summer weeks flew by, and the royal visit drew nearer, he had a thousand and one problems on his mind.

The ordinary building operations had to go forward, so that as much as possible was finished to show off to the King. The damage caused by the fire had to be repaired or concealed. The newly laid-out gardens had to be turfed and planted to look as though they had been there a hundred years. The horses must be exercised and groomed and brought to perfect condition for royal inspection, and the race-course cut through the adjacent woods must be levelled and made fit for galloping.

Apart from all that was involved by the newness of the Castle there were all the elaborate preparations needed for welcoming the sovereign at any time. There was the lodging of their Majesties, the ladies and gentlemen in close personal attendance, the principal court officers, the bodyguard, and a host of menial servants, with all that this implied in food, drink, and fodder for their innumerable horses. Other courtiers, with their own attendants and hangers-on, would have to be accommodated in houses throughout the neighbourhood. Mercifully, the Marquis of Lockerbie would be one of these. Lady Ravenwood could not have stomached his sleeping under her roof, and even Mandeville seemed relieved that their enemy would be lodged two or three miles away.

"Though I think," he said cheerfully, "that we are safer once the King is here. Even Lockerbie's hands are tied then. Any violent attempt, in proximity to His Majesty, would be infinitely more serious."

"It would be treason," agreed Ravenwood. "No, when the King arrives I shall breathe more freely. And *his* safety, thank God, will be the responsibility of his bodyguard."

One way or another, though, his lordship was left with enough responsibilities without being involved in the production of the masque. Anthony could only marvel at the patience with which he listened to the warring partners and sometimes managed to make peace between them.

The shape of the performance was now finally settled, not a day too soon. From the opening antimasque, with its acrobats and tumblers grotesquely guised as Centaurs, to the grand finale when the more courtly performers descended from the stage and chose dancing partners from among the audience, the sequence of episodes, of scene-changes and transformations, was

171

mapped out. It was, Challenor declared bitterly, a travesty of the antique Grecian story. Huntley thought it would make a splendid show and, if any learned scholars were present and distressed by it, well, there was a most convenient river into which they could leap.

On one point there was universal agreement: Ravenwood, the munificent patron of this lavish entertainment, must himself appear in it.

It need be only a token appearance. The main burden of the performance would be borne by the paid actors, dancers and singers, even now on their way down to Herefordshire. But a masque was a court affair, and custom demanded that people of quality participated. Amoret would be among the courtiers who danced the last shadowy saraband and then came down into the audience to set off the general revels. Lady Ravenwood must be another. Other non-speaking parts were provided for Margaret and little Gilbert. Fabian was coming, and would – rather sheepishly, Anthony imagined – take his place among the elegant young noblemen. Mandeville declared himself thankful that, as a mere baronet, he was not invited to join so exclusive a band.

For his lordship a particular, and appropriate, role was reserved.

For the climax of the masque he would take over the character of the hero Bellerophon, portrayed up to that moment by one of the hired players. It was fitting that Ravenwood, so famous for his own horsemanship and stables, should be depicted as the tamer of the immortal Pegasus, descending from the clouds at the conclusion of the saraband and then advancing to the front of the stage to deliver the last eight lines of the poem, a string of effusive compliments addressed directly to their Majesties.

He had no other words to memorise. Quite enough, thought Anthony. Their sugary sweetness was enough to make a man sick.

The lines were nothing. Nor, Huntley assured his lordship, was the impressive entrance. But these things must be rehearsed, and nothing left to chance.

"Then the sooner the better, if your machine is ready," said Ravenwood.

He would have no time later. When the King approached the boundaries of Herefordshire he would have to ride out to meet him with the Lord Lieutenant and other noblemen of the county. Then, after a day-long ride conducting the royal party to Crucorney, he would be at their Majesties' service every waking moment during their stay. While Amoret and her fellow courtiers were free to try on their costumes and run through their scenes, he would be showing off his buildings or the race-course or otherwise playing the attentive host.

So a private rehearsal was arranged, and one evening, after supper, they all adjourned to the Riding House. While Lady Ravenwood and Challenor took their places to judge the effect from below, Anthony followed his lordship and Mandeville, with Huntley and some of his mechanics, up the staircase to the stage-loft.

"It is quite simple, my lord, and quite safe."

Huntley pointed to the great wheel, twelve feet across, fixed horizontally in the centre of the floor, with a complicated pattern of wires and cables attached to it.

"This is the device that I use earlier in the masque, my lord, when the clouds part to disclose the Nine Muses slowly circling through the air. There will be nine harnesses, on strong wires, hanging from the spokes of this wheel, so that as my men turn this capstan, so the Muses revolve."

"I see," said Ravenwood, looking as cheerful as he could.

"For Bellerophon to ride Pegasus, and dismount on the stage, calls for more art. I won't weary your lordship

173

with explanation of the pulleys and winches and—"

"Just tell me what I have to do."

"Here, you see, is our horse, slung by two powerful cables, one at the mane, the other at the tail. There must be two, or it will spin round in the air. The cables look thick, I know, but they will not be seen by the audience – there is only the torchlight far below."

"I care not how thick they are," said his lordship.

"My men will turn you three times, so that the spectators may see you riding high amid the clouds. Then, as they continue to turn the wheel, the two cables will be slowly unwound from that drum – so that you gradually descend, with each revolution of the wheel coming nearer and nearer to the stage until you touch it and are able to dismount. Then," concluded Huntley airily, "you have nothing to do but come forward, make your bow to their Majesties, and deliver your speech. You may need to raise your hand and quell the applause – it is likely to be prolonged, after so ingenious a device. It would be disappointing for Mr Challenor if his verses were not heard."

"It will be disappointing for me if I have broken my neck," said Ravenwood. He climbed gingerly into the saddle of the mythological creature, tested the vital cables fore and aft, and nodded for the men to lower him through the alarming gulf in the flooring.

All, needless to say, went well. Huntley had tested his equipment again and again before risking his patron's life. There were cries of slightly nervous delight from the watchers below as Ravenwood went circling round and round, down and down, to the safety of the stage.

"A good ride," he commented on arrival, "though the beast is somewhat lacking in spirit."

All agreed that it would make an excellent climax to the entertainment, and could not fail to make an impression upon their Majesties.

Ten days later came the royal Harbingers, two gentlemen ushers of the King's Bedchamber, whose function was to announce the impending approach of the entourage and to check that all accommodation was ready to receive them.

It really looked now – though Anthony scarcely dared to say it even to himself – as though the great day were at hand.

Sixteen *Rehearsals*

It felt good, thought Amoret, to be sleeping once more at the Priory after so many nights in strange houses during the long weeks of the summer progress.

Yet at the same time odd, with her host and hostess and her true friends across the river in the Little Castle. This time she must make do with one of the lesser chambers, and share it with several other Maids of Honour, one in the same bed. And the happy atmosphere of a family home, which she remembered for the children's chatter and Lady Ravenwood's kindness and private jokes exchanged with Anthony, had turned to the rigid etiquette which at once took over any building that became the temporary lodging of their Majesties. Armed guards at every turn... Self-important officers strutting to and fro... But at least no ghostly apparitions!

She could see from the start that things were going well. On the morning after the court's arrival they were all conducted round the new castle. In that long straggle of admiring, exclamatory notables it was not hard to lag behind and fall into a low-voiced conversation with Mandeville.

"My lord has made an excellent impression—"

"You think so? It's hard to tell."

"But you know what the King is like, Renold! Few words. And cold. But he speaks more freely to the Queen. And – from what she has let out already – he is charmed. And she too."

"It's to be hoped so. Or all this stupendous cost will have been in vain. Not to mention the risks. Which reminds me – how is our Scottish friend taking it?"

He glanced meaningly up the line ahead of them. Lockerbie was close at the King's elbow as Ravenwood pointed out some architectural embellishment.

"He seems content." She frowned. "He has become very pleasant. There have been no more of those little ill-natured remarks. On the way here, I've even heard him speak well of his lordship. I think he's making the best of it. Perhaps he thinks that if he can't block his lordship's rise it's better to make a friend of him – hope to work together—"

"If he thought he could ever work with Will, he would be a fool indeed. And, whatever else he is, he is not a fool."

"I can only say, he shows no bad humour over the visit here. Watch him. He's smiling and relaxed."

"Which troubles me more than anything. It suggests confidence."

No further talk was possible. A Maid of Honour must not be seen in long private conversations with gentlemen not of the court. Mandeville moved on to greet Endymion Porter, and later she saw him laughing with her brother. That did not matter. Young men together, she thought a little enviously.

The afternoon would be more to Fabian's taste. The gentlemen were going to try out Lord Ravenwood's best running horses on the track he had cut through his woods. The Queen would rest. Those ladies who, like Amoret, were taking part in the masque would be released from attendance so that they could rehearse. Strictly speaking, that was where Fabian should be, but he had stubbornly refused. Another young lord had taken his place in the cast.

The Riding House had been marvellously changed

since her first sight of it several months earlier. Then she had seen a plain, unfinished building designed for utility. Now the high bare walls were draped with hangings of blue and silver. At one end was the richly-painted proscenium arch, the stage behind it hidden by a decorative curtain in panes of primrose yellow and watchet blue. At the other end rose the balustraded scaffold for the most important spectators, with two thrones for their Majesties set on a railed dais in the centre, backed with blue and green velvet all embroidered with crowns and roses. From stage and scaffold alike there were steps down to the polished floor, where humbler guests would stand to see the show, until at the end, when the masquers came down to start the general dancing, they would make way for their betters.

"It is excellently done."

Amoret glanced down to see Zorzi at her side. "You approve?" she said softly.

The midget nodded vigorously. "You know – even before I came to your country – in Italy I have seen many palaces and splendid entertainments. Your Lord Ravenwood has good taste. Or good advisers."

Zorzi was to have his own place in the production, among the musicians. The unearthly music, for certain dramatic moments such as the appearance of Athene, would be provided by his violin.

The Riding House seemed full of people. There were the hired performers, who had already been at Crucorney for some time, drawn apart in their murmuring groups, at the same time deferential and resentful towards the titled amateurs. There were those amateurs, at once excited and striving not to appear so, babbling in high-pitched voices. There were Huntley's stage hands, quiet, serious, patient-looking men with an air of purpose in every move they made. And there were various other folk, among them Anthony Bassey. Their eyes met. They exchanged guarded smiles.

178

Then it was away, back-stage, to the tiring-room (longed-for moment!) to see the costumes and try them on.

Dear Mr Huntley! She forgave him all his gruffness. As a Nymph she was to wear sea green, which always looked well by candlelight, with carnation cloth-of-silver. And for the finale, as promised, aurora colour and cloth-of-gold. Even the dark robes for the saraband were becoming. The starry coronets would flash back the torches. Even now, in the daylight, she could imagine herself as she would appear tomorrow night, illuminated with all the cunning of well-placed lamp and candle and reflector, shining through jars of coloured water that winked like so many rubies and sapphires and emeralds.

In a daze of pleasure she stood patient while a respectful seamstress, with a few deft stitches, took in her bodice for a more flattering fit.

Mr Challenor was tapping on the door. "By your leave, ladies! I am anxious to begin—"

Eventually they all streamed out, laughing or grumbling as the case might be. The rehearsal went on, by fits and starts, through the hot August afternoon. Mr Challenor was supposed to direct the acting, Mr Huntley to be responsible for the effects and such stage movements as were concerned with them. Half the time, inevitably, things were so intermingled that it was hard to say who should have the deciding voice. The Masque of Pegasus, Amoret said to herself, might have been better called the Drama of Cat and Dog.

Zorzi had a less trying time. Provided the musicians came in at the right moment, they had merely to play. The music cues must be noted, to accord with an entrance or some stage effect, and then all should be well.

The mechanical devices delighted the little Italian. They appealed to his quick intelligence. He had always been conscious of the affinity between music and mathematics. He would have given much to talk to this hot-tempered Mr Huntley and ask how he set about devising and calculating the creation of these effects.

In his eagerness, conscious that time was all too short and that tomorrow would be an even busier day, he made a false step. At the end of that exhausting afternoon he approached Huntley and, in his most careful English, offered his congratulations.

"And – if you would permit, signore – I should like much to go up there and see how these wonderful things are accomplished."

He could scarcely have chosen a worse moment. Never the most patient of men, Huntley had endured irritations that had frayed his temper to snapping point. He scowled down at the dwarf as if he could cheerfully have torn him apart with his great hairy hands.

"Well, I *don't* permit. I'll have no one up there monk-eying with my machines. Fiddling about, and putting things out of order."

Later, a much distressed Amoret was to smooth things over as best she could. She would explain to Zorzi that in English "monkeying" was no sneer at his small stature and that people spoke of "fiddling" without any reference to violins. Huntley had many faults but he was kind by nature. He could never have meant to wound Zorzi with personal insults.

At the time, however, the dwarf's English being literal and imperfect, he was deeply hurt. "Your pardon, signore," he said coldly, and walked away with a dignity the King himself could not have bettered. He would not ask this boor again.

Outside the Riding House the day had gone more smoothly.

It was not until Mandeville and Anthony met in the small room they had to share in the Little Castle that they were able to compare notes.

"The horse-racing put everyone in an excellent humour," said Mandeville, "even the gentlemen who did not win – or lost their bets! Our young Lord Grisedale rode well. Sir Thomas beat him only by a short head. The King professed himself delighted with the course. I've never seen him more at ease. Most gracious to Lord Ravenwood."

"He has been singing my lord's praises to the Queen." Anthony explained in a casual tone that he had encountered Amoret as the ladies took the evening air at dusk. She had managed to bring him up to date with the latest gossip in the Queen's apartments.

"Which is?"

"That Her Majesty is as warm as the King. Such a man as my lord should not be left to waste in the country. He should come to court. The Queen urges the King to make him one of his Privy Council. And – if this visit ends as happily as it has gone so far – to advance him in rank. The whisper is, an earldom."

"Indeed?" Mandeville smoothed his moustache thoughtfully. "Our Maid of Honour is useful."

"Useful!" Anthony could not keep his indignation out of his voice. "I'd have said she was more than that. Sir."

"I am sure you would. How went the rehearsal?"

Anthony described the events of the afternoon. "But apart from such hitches," he concluded, "it went very well. So far as the masque is concerned, I think we can rest easy."

"*You* may rest easy. For myself, I think I'll go round my sentries before I come to bed." He sighed. Studying his features in the candlelight Anthony read the familiar signs of tension. Mandeville would not relax until this business was over. "There are too many fresh faces at Crucorney," his master went on.

"I know, sir. I've felt that even in the Riding House. Since all these players and musicians arrived – and now the royal servants – and folk streaming in and out from every corner of the county."

"You've done all you can. And so, I think, have I. The gates are shut. The whole place was searched at sunset. There should be no strangers lurking inside. In daylight it's harder to check – but it's also harder for them to do anything. Even Lockerbie can hardly buy an assassin for a task like this."

"He'd be seized in a moment—"

"Yes. And the punishment would not be pleasant. An attempt on the life of the King's host – even an unsuccessful attempt . . . in a place that ranks, for the time being, as a royal palace, by virtue of the King's presence . . . Not even our crazy Ruthin would try it. Nonetheless," said Mandeville moving to the door, "I'll take the air before I sleep."

Anthony's thoughts flew back to that similar night at the Priory, when Mandeville and Tobias had watched by turns and Ruthin had made his appearance on the roof. But this time there were no nocturnal alarms. He slept undisturbed, waking to a golden summer morning that promised a fine evening for the banquet on the terrace.

There was another rehearsal of the masque in the afternoon. This time it was played straight through, from the rise of the curtain to its fall, without interruption. Everything went straightforwardly. Thanks to the paid performers and musicians, and Huntley's ingenious operators behind the ever-changing scenes – all of whom had been well drilled in their parts throughout the preceding week – the aristocratic amateurs were discreetly shepherded through their episodes without any noticeable disasters.

Even Ravenwood had managed to excuse himself from attending the King for an hour or two, and took his place as Bellerophon in the finale. Anthony noticed that Mandeville had slipped in unobtrusively, and was watching all these antics with a faintly sardonic smile. But at the end, when there was a general hasty exodus, the courtiers mindful that they must dress now for the banquet, Anthony looked for him in vain. He would have liked to hear his opinion. Better, though, to wait until after the performance itself, when all the artifices of lighting had lent their magic to the spectacle.

Zorzi, for his part, was still chiefly intrigued by the mechanics of the show. Prosaic daylight, which gave him at least some glimpse of how the effects were worked, only increased his interest. From his place among the musicians he had seen the ropes and wires which tonight would be invisible, but he was still frustrated, longing for a sight of that mysterious region, high overhead, from which they swung.

No, he would not ask Mr Huntley again...

He lingered while the Riding House emptied. In an hour or two, he guessed, this man would have his mechanics back, checking, adjusting, making everything ready for the performance. But first even these fellows must have some respite.

He waited until he could be certain that no one was still up there in the stage-loft. He crept up a few stairs and listened. There were no voices overhead. No footsteps echoing on the boards. No clicks or creaks from the machinery.

He mounted, slowly and tentatively, the rest of the stairs. He peered round. There were shadowy corners, where canvas clouds and other unidentifiable objects had been pushed to the side-walls until needed. But a clear white daylight poured through the windows, showing up the great central wheel, the winches and cable-drums and counterweights, the dangling harnesses, and all those perilous open spaces yawning between the planks.

It showed too that there was no one there.

He tiptoed carefully across the floor, stepping round

the gaps. Then, for some minutes, he forgot everything else in his eager examination of the machines. His mind raced, trying to fathom how they functioned. It leapt, with sudden intuition, as some complex contrivance gave up its simple secret. Wistfully, he fingered levers that his commonsense warned him not to pull. Probably, almost certainly, the thing worked *so*. But he dared not put his deduction to the test.

Nor must he linger. Life had taught him caution. First, he had been born a midget, subject to constant humiliation and insecurity. If that was not enough, he was now a foreigner in this self-centred, insensitive England. He must not be found alone here, prying into Mr Huntley's precious secrets.

He was about to leave when a faint sound on the stairway froze him into immobility. He had left it too late. Someone was already coming back.

He thought rapidly. He could, of course, brazen it out. If it was not the preposterous Huntley himself, merely one of his assistants – well, he, Zorzi, a violinist in the royal service, a participant in tonight's performance, was guilty of no terrible offence if he came up to the stage-loft for a peep. But it might *be* Huntley, who had refused him permission and insulted him. Better wait and see. He slipped silently into one of the dark nooks between the scenery.

Footsteps mounted the stairs. But they were oddly soft, as stealthy as his own had been a quarter of an hour earlier. It was not the confident tramp of Huntley or his workmen. Zorzi crouched, pressing himself back as far as he could.

Whoever it was, the man paused at the head of the stairs. Zorzi strained his ears for the next move. There were a few creaks, then utter silence. Had the unknown glanced round, seen the loft apparently empty, and gone down again? Or was he still standing there, motionless as Zorzi himself? Unable to bear the suspense, the dwarf thrust his head slowly forward, inch by inch, until he could see. To his relief there was no one there.

He would give the fellow a minute to get clear away, then he would chance his luck no further, but get down those stairs and out of the building before anyone else appeared.

Fresh sounds from below warned him that it was already too late. Footsteps climbing again. These too were furtive. But this time there were whispering voices as well. Two men were creeping into the loft. Perhaps the first man had been down to fetch an accomplice?

"Accomplice" was the word that sprang naturally to Zorzi's mind. This catlike stealth suggested that the men had no more business here than he had. Their motive might be very different from his own innocent curiosity.

It was now even more important not to be seen. There was something to be said for smallness after all.

The men spoke. One said: "Over here."

"No, Sir Dudley. Over here. I can see the horse."

"So can I." This voice was impatient. Though pitched low, it had the ring of command. "It is there for the opening scenes. For the last scene it is unhitched and slung from the other ropes, so that it can move round with the big wheel. If you get the wrong ropes you will kill some poor devil of an actor instead! Ravenwood himself does not take over until the end. It's these two ropes hanging ready above the wheel. The man told us."

"I could scarce make out his London speech," grumbled the other voice. And I, thought Zorzi, can scarce make out yours. The English he had learnt was the English of the court. This broad western pronunciation was hard to follow. "Also," went on the voice, "he was far gone in liquor."

"If he had not been, we couldn't have got him talking at all," said the first man curtly. "Now. Do you see what is to be done?"

"I reckon so. Not that I've ever had aught to do with these stage contrivances—"

"You have been to sea, man. You know one end of a rope from another. You can see where these will run over the two pulleys as they are wound off the drum—"

"Ay, that's plain enough. Let's see now."

"We haven't all day. If we're found up here—"

Very softly – for Huntley never spared the grease – Zorzi heard the cable-drum turning. "Stop," ordered the man addressed as Sir Dudley. "That's enough. The horse will be hanging – what? – seven feet below? If the ropes snap then, just as they unwind off the drum and take the weight—"

"My lord should give you no more trouble." The callous chuckle made the little Italian's flesh creep. "A drop like that. All o' forty feet, I reckon."

"Do it then. Quickly."

There was a new sound, the friction of a knife-blade sawing through strands of rope. Then the gentleman's voice again.

"That's enough, man, or you'll cut right through. With Ravenwood's weight, and the horse itself, that'll snap all right. Now the other rope . . . Get the lengths matching . . . Excellent. Now wind them back, just as they were before. You're sure they'll not break too soon?"

"Trust me, sir. They'll hold till they take the full strain."

"Good. Now let's get out of this place. Separately. I'll see you tomorrow. If it's all gone well, you'll get the rest of your money then."

They spoke no more. First one man, then the other, crept softly down the stairs. Zorzi waited until he judged the coast was clear, then, quivering with pent-up excitement, picked his way across the floor. It was a

wonder that his heart did not stop with the sheer appalling shock when, as he reached the top of the stairs, he
felt a hand clamped suddenly on the nape of his neck.

Seventeen *A Masque to Remember*

One thing seemed certain: the masque at Crucorney would never be forgotten by anyone attending it.

All through the afternoon, on horseback or by coach, the local nobility and gentry streamed in beneath a halcyon sky. Even Lady Mandeville had crossed the hills and blossomed into a grand lady who could hold her own with any of her neighbours. She saw Anthony, beckoned imperiously, and demanded to know where her son was. Anthony had to murmur an apology. His master had great responsibilities today, Lord Ravenwood depended upon him to see that nothing untoward occurred.

She nodded. "I know my son. He's well employed. I shall find him." She sailed on, nodding and smiling to left and right.

The heat of the day was slackening when the trumpets called the guests to the banquet, but the soft air was still warm from the sunbaked walls facing the terrace. There could have been no finer setting, with the distant prospect, the billowing foliage tumbling steeply below the balustrade, and the river flashing white amid its boulders.

Anthony saw little of the banquet itself beyond the unending file of servants who streamed to and fro with tantalising delicacies. That did not vex him. Ravenwood's hospitality was on such a lavish scale that there would be plenty left over and even the humblest would get their share. All had worked hard, and all, vowed his lordship, should enjoy this glorious occasion.

The masque was different. It would be played once, and never again. But what with the extra scaffolds put up along both sides of the Riding House, and the vast standing space on the ground floor, there was room for a numerous company. Anthony made sure of his own place in good time, slipping into the left-hand gallery with a good view one way down on to the stage, and the other way to the thrones on the dais.

Soon, with the banquet over, the guests of quality came flooding in. After a fanfare of trumpets Charles and Henrietta Maria made their stately entrance and were conducted to their seats. The vacant area around them filled quickly with the courtiers of highest degree, the ladies-in-waiting who were not performing in the masque, the gentlemen of the bodyguard.

Anthony identified the tall figure of the Marquis, elegant in cream satin and saffron silk. Very close – as always – to the much smaller figure of the King.

Music played. Most of the lamps and candles were extinguished. The curtain went up, swift and silent in response to Huntley's counterweights. The first scene was revealed, a glowing, sun-drenched Arcady. The Centaurs came galloping in, long tails swishing behind their dappled breeches. Mellow with good food and wine, the audience responded heartily to their acrobatic antics. Roars of laughter greeted their parody of fashionable equestrian evolutions, as they clumsily executed *voltes* and *demi-voltes, caprioles* and *passades*. It was just like my Lord Ravenwood to permit this good-humoured mockery of expert horsemanship.

After the comic relief of the antimasque, everyone settled down happily to the subtler masque itself, with Challenor's high-flown poetry leading on, episode by episode, to ever more breathtaking demonstrations of Huntley's art.

Anthony was as spell-bound as any, though he knew how these magical effects were achieved. As Huntley had promised, the artifice of lighting made all the difference. Now the combination of sight and sound – the clear voices of the singers, the rippling movements of the dancers, the shivery sweetness of the music – these, and all the other elements, combined to create an incredible, heart-piercing beauty.

All the players were masked. But when it was the courtiers dancing, as in the scene of the Nymphs, he could always pick out the slender figure that was Amoret.

Scene followed scene. Very truly "like clock-work", he thought, imagining those rollers winding the canvas landscapes up and down, the prisms pivoting to offer a fresh side, a mountain crag replacing a Grecian temple, an olive-tree after that.

The Nymphs duly gave Perseus his winged sandals. Perseus slew the Gorgon, Medusa, and as the monster sprawled down behind the rocks Pegasus made his first appearance amid ecstatic applause, seeming veritably to be born from the decapitated body. Convincingly life-like, the beast plunged skywards on its invisible wires, and, pausing only to deliver half a dozen of Challenor's surviving lines, the hero rose from the ground in pursuit.

And so it went on. Now Perseus gave place to Bellerophon. He tried vainly to tame the mythical stallion. Exhausted he lay down to sleep – and, as he dreamed, Athene's miraculous materialization evoked fresh raptures from the audience. So too, when the stamp of Pegasus's hoof produced the sacred fountain, Huntley's craft achieved all he had said it would.

The masque was nearing its end. Anthony turned his head to see how the King and Queen were taking it. But the lights now were dimmed for the dance of the shadows – the music had already changed to the

measured rhythm of the saraband – and it was impossible to see the expression on their Majesties' faces. But
the cream satin of the Marquis made him a conspicuous
figure in the gloom. He was leaning forward on his stool
with particular intentness.

Anthony's attention swung back to the stage. This
time even he could not distinguish Amoret among those
mysterious dark-robed shapes moving to and fro in the
light of a few torches. Huntley had devised this most
cunningly. Suspense was building up with each note of
music, each soft footfall. Everyone knew that something was about to happen, though Anthony was one of
the few who knew what. It did not spoil – rather it
enhanced – the sense of exalted anticipation that gripped
him.

The last notes of the saraband died away. The dancers
stood, statuesque in the glimmer. Then a trumpet
pealed. The torchlight strengthened as more blazing
flambeaux swung into position. There was a low
murmur of admiration as the dancers slipped off their
black taffeta robes and were revealed in a brilliance out-
shining all the costumes worn before. Then a gasp of
wonder from the entire audience as, high above the
stage, Bellerophon rode Pegasus against the dark sky.
Circling, and circling again, the hero's gilded armour
flashing back the red glow beneath. Then the clouds
parted and moonlight bathed the whole scene in
silver.

Again Anthony glanced quickly at the royal dais. It
was possible now to see faces. Their Majesties were rapt,
entranced by the spectacle. Lockerbie was almost
crouching. Huntley's art must have cast its spell even on
him.

Three times the rider circled. Then, still circling, he
began to descend. The dancers stood, arms uplifted in
salute. At last the graceful spiral movement brought the
horse to the level of the stage. The rider dismounted

and, amid a positive hurricane of applause, advanced and bowed thrice towards the King and Queen. Peeling off his golden vizard, he revealed his real identity. The familiar voice of Ravenwood rang through the lofty building.

"*Your Majesties, our masquing now is done . . .*"

Challenor's lines rolled smoothly off his tongue. Anthony did not listen again to those sickly, subservient flatteries. It might be the way the court game must be played, but he did not like hearing them on the lips of a man he respected as he did Ravenwood. He looked again at their Majesties. Doubtless, they were lapping up the conventional compliments as their natural due. But what arrested Anthony's attention was the expression on Lockerbie's face. With him too, if only for a few moments, the mask was off. Naked fury worked in his features.

Ravenwood spoke the last rhyming couplet. It was the cue for the musicians to strike up a spirited coranto, signal for the ball to begin. Ravenwood came down the steps to the dancing floor, Amoret and her companions eagerly following. The audience parted to left and right, falling back as the King and Queen led their party down to meet the masquers and choose partners for the dance.

Lockerbie, from habit, kept close behind the King. But he came down the steps like a man dazed from a blow. Or some creation of Huntley's, a bloodless automaton worked by wires.

Their Majesties turned to each other, with solemn bow and curtsey, and led off the dance. After waiting a respectful moment or two, the other principal guests paired off with due regard to etiquette. Lockerbie stepped up to Lady Ravenwood and bowed over her hand, but before she could respond there was a startling intervention.

"I marvel you have the face, my lord – when you have just tried to murder her husband!"

There was no mistaking that voice. Accustomed to addressing her servants and tenants from the opposite side of a field, Lady Mandeville was easily audible above the music and the babble of the company.

Equally audible was the cracking slap of her hand across Lockerbie's frozen features.

There was a horrified hush around them. In a few seconds it spread to every corner of the hall. Even the musicians realised that something extraordinary was happening. The strains of the coranto died limply away.

"Who is this lady?" The King forced out the words with painful hesitancy.

The Scotsman had recovered his normal self-control. "A madwoman, Your Majesty – or perhaps drunk. It is nothing. Let it not interrupt our dance."

"Murder may be nothing to you," said Lady Mandeville implacably. "It is not so in these parts, I tell you."

Two gentlemen of the bodyguard started towards her. She gave them a look that would have halted a charging bull.

"Who is this lady?" the King repeated impatiently.

She answered for herself, swiftly. "I am Lady Mandeville. Of Wildhope."

"My mother, Your Majesty."

For the first time Anthony saw his master below him.

The King paused, looked more indecisive than usual. Clearly the familiar name, and the relationship, checked any impulse to deal too severely with this interruptor.

"M-madam – you have made a serious ch-charge against this gentleman—"

"It is God's truth, Your Majesty. I heard it from my son's lips. Not two hours past."

The King turned to Mandeville. In a low but distinct tone Anthony caught Mandeville's words: "I have proof, sir. There was an attempt on my Lord Ravenwood's life. And my lord Marquis here was behind it."

Now the King sounded thoroughly shaken. "This

must be inquired into—"

There was a flurry of court officers around him. Anthony caught the words "in the morning" but the King was shaking his head vehemently.

"No. Tonight. Or we lose a day on tomorrow's journey."

Anthony judged it time to be at his master's elbow in case he were needed. He pushed his way down the steps and edged his way forward as best he could. He heard the King say, "No, let the dancing go on. It is no fault of my Lord Ravenwood that this has happened. I would not have his entertainment spoiled."

The royal party moved off towards the door. The musicians struck up a coranto again. Anthony managed to pluck Mandeville's sleeve.

"Ah, Anthony! Pat on your cue! Find Zorzi – bring him straight down to the Priory. To the great chamber. My dear mother's temper has somewhat hastened matters. His Majesty vows he won't sleep until he has got to the bottom of this affair. Oh, and – Anthony!"

"Sir?"

"Mr Huntley will be needed too."

Anthony sped off towards the stage, weaving his way through the dancers. At that moment there was a loud explosion outside, followed by a series of lesser bangs. The windows framed the flashes briefly – ice-blue, fire-red, deathly green.

Everyone had forgotten the fireworks that were to round off the evening.

He found Huntley first, busy behind the scenes. The designer did not seem unduly surprised by the summons. "Tonight – now?" he grumbled.

"It is the King!"

"Then I reckon I'll have to. I'd best bring the evidence," he added without explanation. Anthony rushed on to beckon Zorzi from his place among the musicians.

The dwarf too seemed less surprised than he had expected. As they hurried down the hill together, their path lit by the soaring fireworks, the descending showers of gold and silver rain, Zorzi poured out as much of the story as he knew. It was a good deal more than Anthony.

Zorzi had witnessed two men tampering with the cables used in the closing scene. But, unknown to him at the time, there had been another witness. Mandeville had been warned of the suspicious strangers – they had been overheard questioning one of the stage mechanics, after plying him with drink with a generosity that was itself suspicious. Mandeville had hidden in the loft, unaware that Zorzi was there before him.

"It was a little comedy afterwards," said the Italian. "For a moment neither of us knew the other. Fortunate for me – Sir Renold realised at once—" He paused. He did not like to refer too often to his size.

"But – Sir Dudley got away?"

"No, no. Both he and his man were taken when they tried to pass the gates. They are locked up." He laughed. "Signor Huntley would have killed them, I think, for tampering with his wonderful device. But he was happily kept occupied. Everything had to be made safe."

They reached the Priory. There were guards at the door of the great chamber, but they were admitted, being concerned with the inquiry.

The room was filling rapidly. The Queen had taken a chair beside the King and they were talking together in low voices. Amoret, hastily changed out of her stage costume, was one of the three ladies in attendance. The Marquis looked disdainful as he conferred with his cronies. Lady Mandeville, ruffled but perky, like a bird caught in a storm, was justifying her action to her son, who was trying vainly to soothe her indignation into a decorous quiet. Ravenwood stood beside him, grave-faced, not speaking. Lady Ravenwood was not there.

Anthony guessed she was still at the Castle, struggling to be a good hostess to the last and bring the festivities there to a happy conclusion. Not that any of the guests could now be unaware of the scandalous scene that had just been enacted.

Huntley arrived, incongruous in that elegantly attired company, two short lengths of rope looped over one arm. Then came two closely guarded prisoners. For the first time Anthony could study Sir Dudley Ruthin at leisure. A small, dark, nimble man of middle age, with eyes that roved malevolently. A face that suggested cunning rather than intelligence. The face of an obsessed, fanatical man. He had the dress of a gentleman, though his sword had been removed and his sash hung empty. The other man was of a rougher sort, shambling, with a hangdog, hopeless expression.

The King conducted their examination himself, with terse questions that it would have taken a bold liar to parry. Sir Dudley, however, denied everything. Even any acquaintance with his fellow-prisoner, who gave his name as Samuel Parry. But when Mandeville testified that they had been observed together, questioning a stage-hand, and that they had been in the loft tampering with the flying device – evidence supported by Zorzi, with Huntley displaying the ropes, half cut through – Parry broke down completely and confessed his part in the business.

Sir Dudley eyed him venomously, then desperately tried a change of tack. Yes, it was true they had tampered with the ropes. He had denied it only to save this poor fellow, Parry, from punishment. For there had been no question at all of harming Lord Ravenwood's person.

"I wished merely to play a trick upon him," he insisted, "by preventing his appearance in the masque. We meant only to put the device out of action. But the contrivance was so ingenious, we did not understand the mode of working. We did more serious damage than was intended."

Anthony glanced round the faces. He saw no sign of belief in the explanation.

"We shall consider that further," said the King dryly. He looked across at Lady Mandeville. "But I cannot understand, madam, why you should accuse the Marquis of Lockerbie."

Lady Mandeville tossed her head. "He was their pay-master."

"This is delusion, Your Majesty," said the Marquis. "I do not know Sir Dudley Ruthin." He paused a moment. "And I am confident he will swear that he does not know me. And that there has never been any sort of communication between us."

There was a sudden tension in the room. Anthony studied the desperation in Ruthin's eyes. The man must have decided that he would gain nothing by contradicting Lockerbie. Lockerbie certainly meant to save himself. He might save his hireling later, if it could be safely done, but not if that hireling had incriminated him.

Ruthin gulped. "I'll swear to that, Your Majesty. I've had no dealings whatever with his lordship."

The King turned again to Lady Mandeville. "You have made a most serious imputation, madam," he said severely, "against the honour of a great nobleman. Have you any evidence?"

"My son told me. I got it out of him," she said, as if that clinched the matter.

Someone tittered at the woman's simplicity. The King said, "What your son told you is not evidence."

"If you will permit me, Your Majesty – perhaps *this* is." Mandeville stepped forward, holding out a piece of paper. "It was found, some months ago, in Sir Dudley's hat. As to the circumstances on that occasion, there is no lack of witnesses. If they are needed."

The King read the letter with puckered brows. "Y-yes... But it bears no signature, Sir Renold. Are you suggesting that this was a letter from the Marquis? Think before you answer." For so small a man Charles could be formidable when he clothed himself with the terrible authority of his kingship. "You are yourself in great peril. To allege a plot to murder – to bring such an accusation against one of the foremost noblemen in the realm—" He fixed Mandeville with a gaze that commanded the desired reply. "Wild words from a lady may be forgiven – and forgotten. Your own case would be vastly different from your mother's. Wait." He turned in his chair and held out the paper for the Marquis to see. "You did not write this, Lockerbie?"

"Most certainly not, Your Majesty."

"So, Sir Renold, I think you would be wise to withdraw your allegation."

Mandeville was pale in the candlelight. "The truth would not be hard to establish. If the Marquis could be given pen and paper – if he would copy out even the first few lines of this letter—"

There was a general murmur, partly of shock and indignation, partly of agreement. Lockerbie himself exploded with anger.

"This is intolerable! I protest, Your Majesty. Am I required to give an example of my handwriting – like some common forger?"

The King pondered. The silence was unbearable. At last he said, painfully and awkwardly, "No. I will not require it."

"You are most gracious," said Lockerbie triumphantly. "I am content."

It was then that, for the second time in the evening, it was a lady who provided the unexpected intervention.

"Perhaps *I* can save my lord Marquis from the indignity he objects to?" Amoret's voice rang through the great chamber, clear if a little shaky. She was fumbling with her dress. Another piece of paper suddenly flashed white in the glow of the candles. "Here is another letter of his. Your Majesty may care to make comparison."

Eighteen *Echoes of a Dance*

For a few moments the King held the two papers, comparing them. Then, Anthony could see, he became more and more intent upon the one Amoret had passed to him. His expression grew thunderous. His lips moved in some half-suppressed exclamation. He handed the letter to the Queen, who was already leaning towards him with an anxious expression. Anthony caught the words, almost choked with anger:

"This concerns you too, my dear."

The Queen's eyes raced over the paper. She flushed. "One of my own Maids of Honour! This is beyond bearing. A lady under my protection. He must go. Promise me – he must go!"

"No question." The King took back the letter. He turned and thrust it under Lockerbie's nose. "You will not deny you wrote *this*, my lord Marquis? You were at no pains to hide your identity on this occasion. This is a most improper proposal – made to a young lady of Her Majesty's household. You know well enough, we will not permit such conduct at our court."

"Your Majesty, I protest – on my honour—"

"Better not speak of your honour. These letters match. The matter of Lord Ravenwood shall be further inquired into." The King stood up with a weary gesture, holding out his free hand to the Queen. "Take those other men away," he ordered. "It is enough for tonight. As for you, my lord Marquis—" He turned

back to face Lockerbie. "I shall not desire your attendance when we leave tomorrow. I do not wish to see your
face again."

"You are dismissed the court." The Queen was
glaring.

"You will not leave the realm," the King added.
"You had best retire to your estates – until you are sum-
moned to answer any charges made against you."

"Not that any will be," said Mandeville cynically an
hour or two later, as he and Anthony prepared for bed.

Worn though he was by the stresses of the long day,
Anthony was roused to protest. "Surely, sir! With that
evidence! Any jury—"

"You forget. A marquis does not have to face 'any'
jury. He can be tried only by his peers. The case would
be heard in the House of Lords – packed with his friends
and others he can buy. By the time it came to trial, the
rights and wrongs would be forgotten, covered up by
other issues. It would be a vote between Lockerbie's
supporters and his enemies."

Anthony realised that was true. "It's a sad state of
affairs for honest men."

"England is in a sad state. That's why Will Ravenwood's sort are so badly needed on the King's Council.
And now I think we'll see him there. Thank God the girl
had kept that old letter! I said she was useful. It clinched
matters." Mandeville yawned. "Past midnight! We
must get some sleep. We'll have to be stirring early, to
see them on their way."

In the hubbub of the royal departure next morning
Anthony was lucky to snatch even a word with Amoret.
They could only whisper breathlessly at the foot of the
staircase, with servants passing and repassing as they
loaded baggage into the waggons outside.

"You saved the situation last night. That letter—"

She smiled teasingly at his expression. "Written last
year, when I first came to court. I took no notice – he did

not try again."

"Why did you keep it?"

She shrugged. "I hardly know. Then, when all this started – when we met that day at Hampton Court – I realised it might be of service somehow."

"Schemer!" he accused her, but amusedly.

"Of course. I am a lady of the court nowadays."

He looked at her very straightly. "Don't let it spoil you. Please."

"Have no fear," she said. "I must go now, Anthony. You know how the Queen watches over my virtue! Don't look so sad. We shall meet again." She squeezed his hand quickly, and gathering up her skirts ran lightly back upstairs.

An hour later the royal party was off, a multi-coloured serpent of cavaliers and coaches slowly uncoiling from Crucorney and winding its way eastwards.

The last she saw of Mandeville was from the window of the coach as it lumbered out through the Priory gates. He had doffed his hat for the Queen's passing, a few moments before, and his long hair glinted reddish-copper in the early sun. Had he caught her eye? Or was his smile just the quietly amused expression he wore for the court in general and all its follies? She could not be sure. Who could ever be sure, with Mandeville?

Her parting with Lord Ravenwood did not come till the next day, for, along with the Lord Lieutenant and the other principal landowners of the county, he must escort their Majesties until they passed out of Herefordshire. The King had expressed a particular desire for his lordship's company, and they rode side by side for much of the time. Amoret, compelled to pass those hours confined in a bumping coach with half a dozen other ladies, managed none the less to get a private word with him when they halted overnight in Hereford.

"All goes well, my lord?"

"I think so, my dear. His Majesty is most gracious."

"So I hear. Is it true you are to be of the Council? And that soon I must address you as Earl of Crucorney?"

"You hear keenly!" He laughed. "But if Rose and I are to be about the court more often, I trust you will not be over formal."

"I shall certainly find it hard to think of little Gilbert as Viscount Ravenwood."

"Titles are empty things." He spoke casually, but she felt the underlying seriousness. "Better a mere baronet, like Renold, than a marquis I might mention. Come to that, is there a better fellow than young Anthony – even though he live and die plain Mr Bassey?"

"There is not. Not in all England," she said with feeling.

His lordship had been given strong hints, he told her, that he would be ill-advised to press a charge of attempted murder against Lockerbie, who was sufficiently punished by his fall from favour. "In that case," he explained disdainfully, "I'll take no further action against Ruthin and his man. I'll not trouble with the small fry, if the big fish is to go free. What does it matter? I've come to no harm, after all."

He turned back the next evening, when the King drew rein at the Worcestershire boundary to take leave of his loyal subjects in Herefordshire. The coaches drew up behind, the horses thankful for a rest at the top of the long hill, the ladies no less glad to step down and stretch their legs.

Everyone stood chatting on the skyline, the wind fluttering skirts and coats and ostrich-plumes. To that gaping Malvern shepherd up there, thought Amoret, they must look like puppets, brightly dressed yet insignificant against the cloud masses sailing by. She gazed down rather wistfully on the road they had come by, ribboning back into that hyacinth-blue distance that hid Wildhope and Crucorney. One of the other ladies called her. They were all climbing back into their coaches. She ran across the smooth sheep-cropped turf, exulting in the momentary freedom. Then slowed to a more digni-fied gait.

Ravenwood grinned as she passed. "We meet again, soon!"

"I'll look forward," she called gaily.

One must always look forward. And she did not look back again. The King was in the saddle, riding on. Her coach creaked forward behind the Queen's. They were over the Malverns now. The vast Vale of Severn spread its green velvet carpet at their feet, on, on and away to the high-banked horizon of the Cots-wolds. In front lay London again – and who knew what fresh adventures?

Meantime, Mandeville and Anthony had escorted Lady Mandeville home to Wildhope and were making a brief stay there. Brief it would be, Anthony was confi-dent. Already he noted in his master's manner the fam-iliar restive symptoms.

"What happens now, sir?" he ventured to inquire. "Do you think my Lord Ravenwood will be able to accomplish anything? He's certainly in high favour with the King."

Mandeville considered. Then he flung out his hands in a helpless gesture. "God knows. If anyone can talk sense to His Majesty, *he* will. But will the King listen? The next year or two will tell. And if not, God help us all."

He walked to the window and stared out moodily. Huge clouds, dark as slate, were rolling up behind the Black Mountains. And within minutes the first rain-drops were rattling on the panes.

Anthony picked up the lute that stood against the wall. He plucked the strings tentatively, humming softly, trying to pick out the tune that had haunted him these past two or three days.

"Ah," said Mandeville. He turned in silhouette against the pallid daylight, himself a black shadow. "You're playing the saraband."

THE END

Author's Note

Although there is a real place called Llanvihangel Cru-corney it bears no resemblance to the setting of this story, for which I have simply borrowed half of its beautiful name. Similarly my Wildhope Hall and Pendock Hill are imaginary. Also, apart from Charles I, Henrietta Maria, and some briefly mentioned courtiers, all characters – like the events – are fictitious.

That does not mean that they are in every way "unhis-torical". There are many parallels in the life of England in the 1630s, just before the Civil War, and I was particu-larly inspired by my researches into the life of a real character, William Cavendish, first Duke of Newcastle, which I have written in *Portrait of a Cavalier*. He too built a superb new castle on a cliff, where its ruins – including the riding house – can still be visited, but it stands at Bol-sover in Derbyshire. He too, to win the King's favour, put on a staggeringly costly masque, commissioned from Ben Jonson, to entertain their Majesties when they stayed at his older house, Welbeck Abbey, close by. He too had bitter and unscrupulous enemies, though none quite as ruthless as Lord Ravenwood's. I must confess to one deliberate alteration of fact – the garden tower, Mirefleur, which Henry VIII built for secret love-affairs, was actually at Greenwich. For Amoret's con-venience I have undertaken the not very laborious task of removing it to Hampton Court.

G.T.
Colwall, Herefordshire, 1981